# WILD REVENGE

TYSON WILD BOOK TWENTY SEVEN

TRIPP ELLIS

TRIPP ELLIS

## WELCOME

*Want more books like this?*

You'll probably never hear about my new releases unless you join my newsletter.

SIGN UP HERE

# 1

"Tyson, I need your help," a frail voice crackled through the speaker on my phone.

The woman's voice quivered slightly. It was soft and delicate. Tortured. On the verge of cracking up. I hadn't heard the voice in several years, and it never sounded like this. It was always strong, confident, and in control.

Now it was unraveling.

The call was from an unknown number. It came through an encrypted messaging app. The communication was about as secure as you could get—end-to-end encryption. It didn't make a stop on someone else's server. It wasn't stored in the cloud in perpetuity. It couldn't be accessed by a third party. Anyone looking at the call would just see an encrypted data set.

"Quinn?" I asked.

The line was silent.

I continued, "Are you okay?"

I was standing on the aft deck of the *Avventura*, looking out over the inky black water. It was a clear night, and stars sparkled above. The half-moon cast a pale glow over the water.

JD and I had worked for several weeks to prepare the event, but so far, the evening hadn't gone exactly as planned. This phone call was certainly an unexpected turn.

Quinn hesitated. "William's dead."

I cringed, and my stomach tightened. "I'm so sorry. Is there anything I can do?"

"They're trying to kill me," she said, her voice finally cracking up.

I heard her sob on the other end of the line. Then she sniffled and pulled herself together.

"Who's trying to kill you?" I asked.

"I don't know."

"Where are you?"

"I'd rather not say."

The line was about as secure as you could get, but I didn't blame her for not wanting to reveal any sensitive details.

Traffic filtered through, and I heard a distant siren.

"I gotta go," Quinn said. "I'll be in touch soon."

She ended the call before I could ask any further questions.

My mind raced with possibilities. I slipped the phone back into my pocket, wondering what the hell was going on.

JD saw the look on my face and knew instantly something was wrong. "What's up?"

I shrugged. "An old friend is in trouble."

That hung in the night air for a moment. Something told me that trouble was heading our way.

I filled JD in on the brief conversation.

He was decked out in a black tuxedo with a cummerbund and bow tie. It was unusual attire for him. His long blond hair was pulled back into a tight ponytail, and he looked rather presentable.

Our guests mingled around the superyacht in evening wear, dressed to the nines. The men were all wearing standard-issue black tuxedos, and the women wore sparkling sequins and fitted black dresses with exposed backs and plunging necklines. Diamonds shimmered around elegant collarbones and dangled from pierced ears. Long-stem champagne glasses swung from perfectly manicured fingers, and the bubbly liquid seemed to evaporate quickly.

Waitstaff hustled about replacing empty drinks with full glasses, serving hors d'oeuvres. A cellist provided the ambiance, filling the superyacht with classical music. A display table showcased the finest gems in Coconut Key—diamond rings, necklaces, bracelets, brooches, earrings.

But it was all an illusion.

Nothing was real. Not even the champagne.

The guests were all undercover deputies, and the sting was a joint operation with the Coast Guard. Waiting in the wings, over the horizon, were several patrol boats ready to swoop in at a moment's notice. The helicopter unit, *Tango One*, was on standby.

The event had been weeks in the making. We'd recruited a local boutique jeweler to go along with the ruse. It was promoted as an exclusive, invite-only showing of the finest and most expensive jewelry available on the island. The phony event was publicized on social media, and we recruited several prominent influencers to partake in the deception. They posted about their plans to attend and purchase high-end jewelry. It was also an opportunity for them to virtue-signal about the silent auction for a stunning piece of jewelry—the proceeds of which would be donated to charity. They posted pictures of the jewelry to be shown, along with mentioning the exorbitant prices.

It was a little plot JD and I had cooked up to draw out the pirates that had been knocking off luxury yachts in the area. With a target like this, who could resist?

That was my thought, anyway.

Of course, the influencers, and the fine jewelry, stayed on the island. The deputies, and the cubic zirconia, did a good job of looking like the real thing—a bunch of trust fund babies with too much money out on the water, mixing and mingling.

A prime target.

But we'd been out on the water since the late afternoon, and despite having excellent bait, we weren't getting any hits—not even a nibble.

Maybe our trap was too obvious?

It had been a while since the pirates struck. Perhaps they moved on to other waters? They were trained professionals. There was no doubt about it. They were efficient and precise. Like a surgical strike team, they masqueraded as Coast Guard with a patrol boat painted to match. They'd board unsuspecting superyachts and rob them blind. They were in and out in a matter of minutes. So far, no one has gotten hurt.

They pretty much stuck to taking jewelry, cash, and other high-value assets like art or rare musical instruments. They were stealing from people who weren't going to put up a fight. The valuables were insured, and the machine guns the thugs carried were enough to keep the rich socialites from sudden bouts of bravery.

Sheriff Daniels looked at his watch and frowned. Even he was dressed in a tuxedo—a rare sight, indeed. "If your pirates don't show up within the next hour, I'm shutting it down."

"I thought for sure this would be too good an opportunity to pass up," I said.

"Maybe one of your influencers spilled the beans, and word got out this was a sting," Daniels said with a tight face.

I shrugged.

We had a slight operational security problem in the department. Paris Delaney, a local investigative journalist, had a source within the department. She seemed to know things the instant they happened. If she was able to get information, others were as well. But we hadn't been able to pinpoint the source of the leak.

We mixed and mingled for a while, pretending to enjoy ourselves. When my eyes weren't ogling Denise, they were scanning the horizon. She looked damn good in a black evening gown that hugged her petite form. Her low-cut neckline was magnetic. And the sparkling diamonds made her look even more regal—even if they were fake. Her flowing red hair shined, accentuating her creamy skin and sculpted cheekbones. The real gems were her emerald eyes.

Despite the glittering bounty, the pirates never materialized. Daniels eventually called the operation off, and we headed back to Coconut Key.

With JD at the helm, the superyacht carved through the swells. Our backup waiting in the wings moved on, and Tango One returned to base. There was a part of me that figured the pirates might pick this moment to strike.

## 2

W e'd just gotten back to the marina at *Diver Down* and connected shore power and water when Daniels got the call. A grim look washed over his face as a deputy gave him the news. "Alright, I'll be right there." He ended the call and slipped the phone back into his pocket. His eyes found mine. "Duty calls, gentlemen."

"What's going on?" I asked.

"There's been an incident on Starfish Key island."

He pulled off his bow tie and unbuttoned his shirt collar as he marched across the aft deck to the passerelle.

JD and I exchanged curious glances.

Waitstaff cleaned up, and the crowd was in the process of dispersing. The owner of the boutique jewelry store collected the fake items and packed them away.

Daniels looked back at us as he reached the dock with an impatient look on his face. "Are you coming?"

"Right behind you, boss," I said.

He gave me a stern gaze before marching down the dock toward the parking lot.

I thanked the boutique owner for her assistance, told the catering company to bill the county, then hustled across the gangway.

"I want to go," Denise said, scurrying after us, her high heels clacking against the deck.

I called Teagan and asked her to lock up the boat after everyone had left. She had a spare set of keys, and I figured it would be easy for her to slip out from behind the bar at *Diver Down* and wrap things up. She'd been looking after Buddy and Fluffy while we were out on the water. I didn't want them anywhere near the action if things went down. They were currently lounging in the loft above the restaurant.

Daniels didn't bother to wait for us. He hopped into his patrol car and took off. The three of us climbed into Denise's banana yellow SUV and followed after him.

JD's face crinkled shortly after he closed the door and buckled his seatbelt. He sniffed twice. "What's that smell?"

"Ugh," Denise groaned. "I can't get rid of it. It's all Tyson's fault."

I raised my hands innocently. "The hazards of the job."

Denise scowled at me playfully.

We'd gone on a trash dive to recover evidence on a previous case, and some unknown substance must have leaked out of the trash bags we put in the back of her vehicle.

"Take it to Tommy at *Coconut Clean,"* JD said. "He'll take care of you. This thing will look and smell brand new when he's finished detailing it."

"I'll pay for it," I said. "It was my idea in the first place."

Denise smiled.

"Police work isn't always glamorous. I'm just saying..."

We pulled into the parking lot of the Sheriff's Office and hustled down the dock to the patrol boat. We met Brenda, the medical examiner, along with a forensics team, and climbed aboard the aluminum vessel. Daniels cranked up the outboards, and the water roiled.

We cast off the lines and idled out of the marina. Daniels throttled up when we cleared the breakwater, bringing the boat on plane. The aluminum boat skimmed across the surface of the black swells as we headed into the night. The engine howled, and mists of saltwater sprayed.

"How was your party?" Brenda asked.

I just shook my head.

"Don't worry, they'll strike when you least expect it."

I sighed. "That's always the way, isn't it?"

It took 20 minutes to get to Starfish Key. It was one of many small private islands. Large enough to build a mansion, ensconced by trees, and have secluded beaches all to yourself. The owner had built a dock and dredged a small canal to accommodate his 92-foot yacht. It was a SunTrekker with windswept lines and luxury appointments.

The *incident* became apparent as we drew closer to the dock.

A bloody body lay motionless, and a frantic man hovered nearby. He paced back and forth. He waved us in, and I tossed him the line. He tied off the boat, and we climbed onto the dock.

The forensics guys immediately started snapping photos and documenting the scene. The camera flashes illuminated the red blood and bounced off the neighboring yacht. Waves lapped against hulls, and a gentle breeze blew across the water.

I asked the man on the dock, "What happened?"

His round eyes darted about, and he fidgeted nervously. He was in his early 30s with dark hair that fell into his face. He wore designer sneakers, a T-shirt, and jeans—a deceptively simple outfit that was outrageously expensive. He wore a fair amount of bling—gold chains, a few diamond rings, and an expensive watch. "I was in the studio when I heard gunshots. I ran out to see what was going on. Sledge was dead."

He motioned to the body.

"Sledge?"

"MC Sledge." He looked at me in disbelief. "Have you been living under a rock? He's got the number one song on the rap, hip-hop, and pop charts right now."

"Okay, now I know who you're talking about," I said, putting it all together. I didn't really follow the genre closely. "And who are you?"

His face crinkled again, and he scoffed. "Shit... I'm Lucas Keys."

The name didn't ring a bell.

He just shook his head, then looked at JD. "You're the singer for Wild Fury."

JD nodded.

"How is it that I know who you are, and you don't know me?"

JD shrugged and smiled.

"What's your relationship to the victim?" I asked.

"I'm his manager and producer. All those number one singles he had... *Money Ain't Shit, Tushy Groove, Next, Suck It, Get Out Alive*... I co-wrote," Lucas said, tapping his chest with pride.

"So, you were in the studio, working on music, I assume?"

"We got a new track that is fire. *Take'n Care of Business.* It's gonna totally kill."

He cringed, regretting the choice of words.

I glanced at the remains. MC Sledge was peppered with gunshot wounds that had oozed blood, soaking his solid white shirt, making it completely red.

Brenda snapped on a pair of pink nitrile gloves and hovered over the body.

"When did this happen?" I asked.

"Maybe 40 minutes ago," Lucas said. "I called 911, and here you are."

"Did you see who did this?"

Lucas shook his head. "Like I said, I was all the way back at the house. The studio is soundproof, so I barely heard the shots. *Clackity, clack, clack!* It took me a minute to realize what it was. Then I ran outside and sprinted to the dock. I heard outboard engines, but I really couldn't tell you much about the boat. I didn't have my glasses. I'm nearsighted. I just saw this fuzzy speedboat disappear into the night."

"You touch the body?"

There were footprints in the blood on the dock. They tracked away from the body and followed the pattern of Lucas's pacing.

I noticed specks of blood on the sides of his shoes.

"Yeah. I knelt down beside the body and checked for a pulse. But he was gone by the time I got here."

The hull of the yacht was peppered with slugs that had missed the intended target. The forensics guys snapped photos. They would dig out the slugs and bring them back to the lab for analysis.

"Looks like a 9mm," Brenda said as she examined the body. "I'll know more later."

"Does he have a phone in his pocket?" I asked.

After patting him down, Brenda said, "No."

She pulled a wallet, keys, and a money clip from his pocket. The clip contained several crisp $100 dollar bills.

"Man, this is so messed up," Lucas said, gazing at his dead friend.

"Do you know where his phone might be?" I asked. "I'd like to see his call logs."

Lucas shrugged. "It might be back in the studio."

"What was Sledge doing out here?"

Lucas hesitated and shifted uncomfortably. "I don't know."

He knew.

I gave him a look that demanded an answer.

"Okay, but you're not gonna bust me, are you?"

I lifted a curious eyebrow. "If you didn't kill anybody, I'm not going to bust you."

"I didn't kill nobody, I swear!" He paused. "Sledge was going to the boat to get a little *herbal inspiration* if you know what I mean."

I knew what he meant.

"We always like to smoke a fat one before we get into a deep session. Helps chill things out. It's like a brain tonic. Stimulates ideas." Lucas shook his head in disgust. "Can't believe Sledge got killed because of a joint."

"Do you have any idea who did this?"

Lucas shrugged.

"Can you think of anybody who wanted to harm Sledge?"

## 3

"**E**verybody who's anybody has got haters," Lucas said.

"Any *haters* in particular spring to mind?" I asked.

Lucas thought about it for a moment. "That little punk bitch DJ Spinx. Maybe he did this." He paused. "Could have been Darius Creel. Could have been Kane and the Dragon Nation."

Dragon Nation was an up-and-coming gang in the area. At least, they wanted to be. They had a website, a social media presence, and even sold T-shirts with their logo, along with other merchandise. But mention their name to a cartel member, and you'd get an eye-roll.

"Sounds like Sledge knew how to make friends," JD said, his voice thick with sarcasm.

"If you don't got haters, you ain't doing it right," Lucas replied.

"Tell me about DJ Spinx," I said.

Lucas grunted. "I'll bet it was that mother fucker."

"Did they get into some type of altercation?"

"You could say that. Sledge discovered him. We was trying to mentor him. Give the kid a shot. That's how Sledge was. He always wanted to give back. Somebody gave Sledge a break. He figured he should do the same. That's how it works, man. Pay it back, pay it forward."

"So what happened?" I asked.

"That ungrateful little bitch stabbed him in the back. That's what. Sledge brought Spinx into the studio. Helped him record a few demos. The tracks were okay, but nothing special. The kid couldn't handle the pressure. Started stuttering. And when he *did* get the lyrics out, his delivery wasn't good. He had no flow. His shit was stale. It happens to some people. They're great when nobody's watching. Shine a spotlight on them, and they shrink. Spinx was always making excuses, too. He drank too much and did too many substances. A lot of people are afraid of success, and they self-sabotage. Anyway, the cat had the nerve to say that Sledge stole one of his songs. Sued him for copyright infringement. If you listen to the tracks, they're nothing alike. He's just an insignificant little man trying to cling onto greatness."

"What's DJ Spinx's real name?" I asked.

"I think it's Charles. Charles Bradford."

I made a note on my phone. "Do you mind if we take a look around the studio?"

"Uh, sure," Lucas stammered.

He led us down the dock, through a path ensconced by trees to a clearing. There was a massive pool surrounded by lounge chairs and swaying palm trees. The swim-up bar would provide guests with a cocktail of their choosing without having to leave the comfort of the water. The two-story house was an architectural masterpiece. Large floor-to-ceiling windows blended indoor and outdoor spaces. There were sharp lines and graceful curves. It looked like it belonged in a magazine and had a mid-century modern vibe reminiscent of the stylish Hollywood homes designed by John Lautner.

Lucas led us around the pool to the two-story guesthouse that had been converted into a recording studio. We pushed inside, and the place reeked of saturated marijuana smoke from years of consumption. The control room had a mixing board with knobs and faders. Big studio monitors pumped out crystal clear sound. There were racks of electronic sound processing gear—vintage preamps, reverbs, compressors, and other effects. There were keyboards and synthesizers. In a soundproof recording bay, there was a full drum set. An isolated vocal recording booth eliminated unwanted frequencies and sound reflections. There were racks of guitars, basses, amps, and cabinets that would fill any musician with envy.

JD's eyes lit up at the sight of all the toys. He was like a kid in a candy store. "Impressive. I definitely need to get me one of these."

Lucas smiled. "MC Sledge's last album went platinum. You know how hard it is to sell a million copies in the age of streaming?"

JD had visions of rock 'n' roll stardom in his eyes.

I looked around the studio, taking in the mixing console, searching various nooks and crannies. There were plenty of empty whiskey bottles in the trash can and the remnants of a marijuana cigarette in an ashtray. There was a large bong on the mixing console.

I didn't see Sledge's cell phone anywhere. "Do you think he left his phone in the main house?"

Lucas shrugged. "Honestly, I didn't really pay any attention."

"What's upstairs?"

"That's where I live. I mean, I keep an apartment on the island, but I'm always here working on tracks."

"What happens to all of this now?" I asked.

Lucas shrugged. "I don't know. Hadn't really thought about it until you mentioned it. The whole estate will probably go to Talia. Guess that means I'll be moving out soon."

"Do you two not get along?"

"I stay neutral. I learned a long time ago that you don't get involved in a man's personal business. You listen to your friend bitch about his wife, but you never talk shit about her 'cause they just might get back together. Then you're the asshole. Know what I mean?"

We both nodded.

"You mind if we take a look upstairs?" I asked.

His brow knitted together. "Wasn't really expecting company."

"It's okay. We won't judge."

"I don't really see the point," Lucas said.

"Maybe Sledge left his phone upstairs."

"Sledge never goes upstairs. It's my personal space. But, if you want to take a look, go ahead."

I smiled. "We'll just be a minute. We won't disturb anything."

"Have at it, kid."

We climbed the steps, and Lucas followed.

It was a nice place. There was an open living room with modern leather furniture, a glass coffee table, a flatscreen display, and a surround-sound stereo system. There was a full kitchen with shiny stainless steel appliances, a laundry closet with a stackable washer and dryer, and a bedroom with a full bath.

I gave a cursory glance around, looking for Sledge's cell phone, but I didn't see it. I kept an eye out for anything suspicious—weapons, blood-stained clothing, etc.

"Anything else you'd like to see?" Lucas asked, trying to hide his irritation.

"I'd like to take a look around the main house."

Lucas nodded and led us downstairs. We marched around the pool to the main house. It was just as beautiful on the inside as it was on the outside.

MC Sledge, or whoever he hired to decorate, had good taste.

Large oil paintings hung on the wall. There was a large styl- ized portrait of the rapper in the living room painted by an up-and-coming pop artist named *Spaz*. There were platinum records on the walls. The kitchen was decked out with state-of-the-art appliances and marble countertops.

The house was fully automated and voice-activated. The lights would turn on, sensing your presence when you walked into a room. You could issue verbal commands to set ambient light, temperature, and turn on music. Speakers were embedded throughout the home and controlled via an iPad or voice. There was a weight room with a treadmill and an exercise bike along with racks of free weights. Sledge had a theater room with posh seating and a large projection screen. If you got bored, there was a game room with a pool table, darts, and stand-up arcade games. When you wanted to entertain your friends, there was a built-in club complete with a stocked bar, stage lighting, a massive sound system, and even a stripper pole and stage for when things got lewd.

It was the ultimate party pad.

"I have definitely got to get me one of these," JD said. "Can you imagine?"

I nodded. "Yes, I can."

JD muttered in my ear. "It might be coming on the market soon."

I had no doubt the home would be listed in the eight-figure range.

During our casual tour, I didn't see any sign of Sledge's cell phone. It seemed unusual that he didn't have one on him at the time of death, but maybe he was trying to disconnect and get into a creative, distraction-free zone.

When we returned to the dock, I took a quick glance around his yacht but came up empty-handed.

Sledge had an expensive watch on his wrist, gold chains around his neck, and a pocket full of cash. This was no robbery. And if someone shot him from the water, I doubted they'd take the time to climb out of the boat and onto the dock just to steal his cell phone and leave his jewelry behind.

"Who's Darius Creel?" I asked.

"He owns Real Creel Records." Lucas shook his head. "Fucking snake. He owes us so much money. We are suing him for unpaid royalties right now. That's motive right there, isn't it?"

"Could be," I said.

"We were trying to get out of the contract. It was a terrible deal."

"You were Sledge's manager. Why did you let him sign such a bad deal?"

Lucas didn't like that. His face tensed. "When you're a nobody, you take what you can get. Hell, I didn't know what I was doing when we signed the contract."

"Then why did Sledge take you on as his manager?"

"Because we're best friends. That's my boy," he said, pointing to the corpse. "We been tight since high school. I always knew Sheldon was gonna make it."

"Sheldon?"

"That's his real name. Sheldon Livingston. I just knew he was gonna be larger-than-life. Turns out I was right."

"What's his beef with Kane and the Dragon Nation?"

Lucas sighed and shook his head in disgust. "Those guys are a joke, and we made the mistake of getting involved with them."

"In what capacity?" I asked.

"We put them in a couple of music videos. We thought it would be good branding for Sledge. Give him that hard-core gangster image. We didn't realize they didn't have much going on. Those guys are LARPing."

"LARPing?"

"*Live action role playing.* They think they're in a fucking video game. Pretend gangsters. But they do a good job of making themselves look fearsome online. It sold a lot of records. Suburban kids see the gangs, the guns, and the booty in the videos and buy the records. They don't know what's legit and what's not. It's all smoke and mirrors. But when Sledge blew up, the Dragon Nation wanted something in return. Said they *made* him. Wanted a percentage of the royalties from those songs. Sledge told them to go fuck themselves. Not in so many words, mind you. He was a little more diplomatic than that. As a concession, he promised Kane that he would cut a track with him, and Kane could split the royalties."

"So Kane fancies himself a rap star?"

Lucas rolled his eyes. "Shit, he can't rap worth a damn. Real pitchy, and he ain't got no delivery."

"Sledge brought him into the studio?"

Lucas nodded. "We cut a couple tracks with him, but they were god-awful. Unbelievable. Sledge didn't want to put them out. Said it wouldn't be good for his brand. He tried to tell Kane the same thing. He told Kane he didn't want those released. It would make Kane look bad. And it would have. That pissed Kane off. Sledge even gave him the original masters so he could do whatever he wanted with them, but Kane wanted them released through the label and with a big marketing push. I mean, it's kind of crazy when you think about it. If you're doing illegal shit, you don't want to attract attention to yourself. But Kane is a fame whore. And I think he started to believe his own hype."

"What is he into?"

Lucas shrugged. "You know, he and his crew make moves here and there, trying to work their way up the food chain."

"Drugs?"

"Drugs, extortion, whatever," Lucas said.

"Was there anyone else on the island at the time of the murder?" I asked.

Lucas shook his head. "Just me and Sledge."

"What about his wife or maybe a girlfriend?"

"Soon to be ex-wife," Lucas said. "She hasn't been here in a long time."

I lifted a curious eyebrow. "Tell me about that situation?"

## 4

L ucas shrugged. "You know how it is. This is a tough life when it comes to maintaining a relationship."

"So, Sledge was fooling around?" I asked.

Lucas shrugged sheepishly. "I mean, a man's gotta do what a man's gotta do, right? When girls are throwing it at you, are you gonna turn it down? You know what the girls look like around here. Ain't enough willpower in the world to resist some of these cuties. And one is never enough." He paused. "But I know Talia. She's a good woman. She's not behind this if that's what you are thinking?"

"Spouses are always considered possible suspects," I said. "It looks like Sledge did well for himself. Divorces can be messy sometimes."

"Murder can be messier," Lucas said. His eyes gazed back to his friend.

"You have contact information for Talia?"

He nodded and texted me her information along with DJ Spinx's, Darius Creel's, and Kane Romo's. "You're gonna catch who did this, right?"

"We're gonna do everything we can," I assured.

"That's my best friend laying there. This shit can't go unanswered," he said, his eyes brimming.

"Just leave it to us. Don't do anything stupid."

"I ain't gonna do nothing stupid. Do I look stupid?"

I didn't answer.

I handed him my card and said we'd be in touch.

Daniels called for a dive team to search the area near the dock, looking for shell casings. It was a long shot, but a stray casing might have fallen into the water.

It was the wee hours of the morning by the time we wrapped up at the scene. Sledge's body was loaded aboard the patrol boat, and we headed back to Coconut Key. The dive team was able to recover a single shell casing from the sandy bottom, but I doubted the lab would be able to pull a print.

It was late by the time we got back to the station and even later when we finished filling out after-action reports.

Denise drove us back to *Diver Down* after we finished up. The bar was closed, and the parking lot relatively empty. JD's Miami Blue convertible Porsche sat alone under a glowing mercury vapor light that bathed the parking lot. Moths and insects buzzed around the light.

"I'll pull phone records tomorrow and see what I can find," she said. "Thanks for letting me tag along."

"Anytime," I said with a smile.

JD and I hopped out of the SUV and watched Denise drive out of the parking lot.

JD looked tired. "I don't know about you, but I'm beat. I'll catch you in the morning," he said as he ambled toward the Porsche.

He clicked the alarm, and the lights flashed. He slipped behind the wheel and cranked up the engine. Classic rock blasted through the speakers. He pulled out of the lot and gunned it as he turned onto the highway. The engine howled, echoing through the night air.

I ambled down the dock to the *Avventura*, checking my phone along the way.

There were no calls from Quinn.

I'd be lying if I said I wasn't worried about her.

I had gotten a text message from Teagan saying she would keep the animals at her place for the night. It was too late to text back. But she was probably still awake, having closed the bar an hour ago.

I crossed the passerelle to the aft deck of the *Avventura*, slid open the glass door, and stepped into the salon. Despite having a faux party, the boat was spotless. The catering crew had cleaned up, and the participants left things as they found them. An unusual situation, considering most of our parties left the boat trashed with beer cans, empty bottles, and articles of clothing.

I made my way to my stateroom on the bridge deck, brushed my teeth, peeled off my clothes, and fell into bed.

The morning sun blasted through the windows all too soon. I pulled myself out of bed and checked my phone on the nightstand—still no message from Quinn.

After breakfast, I called JD. He swung by the marina and picked me up. I hopped into the convertible Porsche, and we cruised over to the *Trident Towers*. According to Lucas, Talia had been living in the luxury highrise since the separation. There was an attached marina filled with luxury yachts and sailboats. Gulls hung in the air, and the morning sun glistened the water. JD parked the car, and we walked to the main entrance.

A quick flash of my badge and the concierge let us into the secure lobby. By this point in time, the cute blonde was familiar with us. The *Trident* was mostly filled with young hip professionals. But it was also home to a few celebrities, sports figures, and some of Coconut Key's wealthy drug traffickers. As with any piece of high-end real estate, there were a lot of units purchased with cash. Real estate had become a great way to launder money with funds transferred from offshore shell accounts and various other concealment schemes.

We strolled across the opulent lobby to the elevator bank and pressed the call button. We took the elevator to the 22nd floor, stepped off, and ambled down the hallway. We banged on the door to suite #2209. It was still early, and I hoped we'd catch Talia at home.

There was no response, so I banged again.

It took a few minutes for her to make her way to the door. "Who is it?"

The peephole flickered as she peered through it.

I held my badge up. "Coconut County. We'd like to talk to you for a moment."

"What's this about?" she asked in a suspicious voice.

"Has anyone from the department contacted you yet?"

"No, why?"

"I'm sorry to be the one to tell you, but Sheldon Livingston is deceased."

She pulled open the door, her jaw slack, her eyes wide. "What!?"

"He was shot last night."

"By whom?"

"We don't know yet."

"What happened?" There was genuine curiosity in her face. Her eyes darted about as she processed the information.

It usually took a minute for the news to sink in and for the waterworks to begin.

Talia was a gorgeous young woman—golden blonde hair, brown eyes, creamy skin. She wore a T-shirt and boy-shorts. Her hair was tousled, and we had clearly awoken her. She didn't have any makeup on, but she didn't need any. Talia was a natural beauty. She had a petite little figure with all the requisite curves. With a woman like that, you'd think MC Sledge would have no reason to stray.

"May we come in?" I asked.

Talia nodded, still in a daze. She stepped aside and motioned for us to enter. She closed the door behind us and escorted us down the foyer into the living area. It was a nice open space with floor-to-ceiling windows and a terrace that looked out over the water. The condo was a one-bedroom with an open floor plan and a modern kitchen—a luxurious apartment by any standards, but certainly not in the same league as a private island paradise.

Talia's eyes brimmed, and she wiped them with the back of her hands. She fumbled for a tissue, grabbing a box from the glass coffee table. She offered us a seat on the sofa. We obliged, and she curled up into a comfy chair, blotting her eyes.

"When did this happen?"

"Last night between 11 PM and midnight," I said.

"Where?"

She was asking all the right questions. That, or she was putting on a good act. I start to get suspicious when people don't ask for details about how a loved one passed.

"At Starfish Key," I said.

Her face crinkled with confusion. "You mean, somebody came to his home and gunned him down?"

"Something like that."

"Who would do that?" she asked.

"That's what I'm hoping you can tell us."

## 5

Talia looked baffled. "I don't know. I mean, Sheldon could be difficult at times. He rubbed a lot of people the wrong way. He had a strong personality. But that's what made him a star. He could be uncompromising when it came to his art. And to anything else."

"You filed for divorce, correct?" I said.

She nodded.

"Care to tell me why?"

"It wasn't just one thing. But I got to the point where I just couldn't deal with it anymore. It all boiled over. I mean, how many times am I supposed to look the other way when he bangs some groupie?"

"I take it that happened a lot?"

She nodded. "I mean, look... I'm not stupid. I know that goes with the territory. But I met Sheldon before he was *Sledge*," she said in air quotes. "He didn't have two nickels to rub together. I didn't marry him for the money."

Her eyes brimmed, and tears rolled down her cheeks. She wiped them away, sniffled, and took a moment to recompose herself.

"I stood by him and encouraged his career," she continued. "I even stood by him when those accusations were made. Then, when our relationship went to shit, I got left in the dust."

"Accusations?"

She groaned and rolled her eyes. "I'm sorry, but that girl was full of shit."

"What girl?"

"Do you guys not watch the news?"

I glanced at JD. He shrugged.

"We must have missed it," I said.

"Your department investigated it," she said.

"We mostly handle homicides," I replied.

"Well, nothing came of it anyway. Sheldon settled out of court. It was just a money grab." She took a deep breath. "Sheldon may have been a lot of things, but he wasn't a rapist."

That hung there for a moment.

"Tell me what specifically happened," I said.

Talia sighed. "He was trying to help the girl. She reached out to him on social media and sent a few videos of her singing. Sheldon was impressed. The girl could sing. I'll give her that. Sheldon always felt like he owed the community. So he gave her a shot. Brought her into the studio, and they recorded a couple of songs. He gave the demos to Darius, but Darius didn't think the girl was anything special, and that was the end of it. It wasn't long after that when she said that Sheldon forced himself on her."

"Where did this alleged assault take place?" I asked.

"In the studio, supposedly."

"Where were you at the time?"

"That was before we separated. I was still living on the island. I met the girl. She seemed nice. Cute. But there's no way in hell Sheldon would bang a 16-year-old girl in the studio with me in the main house. Even Sheldon wasn't *that* stupid."

I exchanged another glance with JD.

"I remember something about that now," Jack said. "She waited several months after the alleged event to make a complaint, right?"

Talia nodded. "There was no physical evidence. Your sex crimes unit came out here and talked to both Sheldon and me. The girl's father filed a civil suit, and Sheldon settled. He didn't want the hassle of going to trial and didn't want the negative publicity. Being a gangster is one thing, but being a creepy pedo is another. It doesn't sell records."

"What did he settle for?"

"$1,000,000. Sheldon wrote a check, and that was it. The girl took down all of her nasty social media posts. All of her videos making unfounded allegations. Sheldon hired a PR firm to scrub all the references from the Internet. It faded away pretty quickly. Now that I think about it, I'm actually not that surprised you guys don't remember it. Sheldon spent a lot of money to make it go away."

"And you still believe Sheldon was innocent?"

She thought about it for a moment. "Yeah, I do. I know Sheldon pretty well. There were lines he didn't cross." She paused. "But I guess people can always surprise you."

A glum silence hung in the room.

"What's the girl's name?"

"Kayla Cross."

"Do you know her father's name?"

"Lincoln."

I made notes on my phone.

Talia blotted her eyes again.

"So, your relationship survived that incident," I said. "What was the final straw?"

"I don't really know. Things had gotten bad between us toward the end. Really bad. It wasn't all his fault. I'll take my share of the blame." She paused, losing herself in thought. "We got into a fight one night. I don't even remember what started it. I just blurted out that I wanted a divorce."

"How did Sheldon feel about it?"

She cringed. "He was not a happy camper. He just couldn't understand why I wanted to leave. As if I was supposed to put up with all his nonsense."

"Did he ever get violent?"

Her face twisted with confusion. "With me? No. But he sure did threaten to put me through hell with this divorce. And he was doing a damn good job of that."

"I have to ask... Where were you last night?"

Her face crinkled. "Do you think I had something to do with his death?"

"It's a standard question, Mrs. Livingston."

"I was out with a girlfriend last night."

"Can you give us her information?"

"Naomi Bowser. You want her phone number?"

I nodded and told her to text the contact information to me. I gave her my number, and the info buzzed my phone a moment later.

"What did you and Naomi do last night?" I asked.

"We had dinner at Blowfish, then we hit a couple clubs on Oyster Avenue. I think I got back here a little after 2 AM."

"Where did you go?"

"We started at Keys, then went to Bumper and danced for the rest of the night."

"What are your thoughts about Lucas?"

## 6

"I think Lucas is a good guy," Talia said. "Great producer. He's done a lot for Sledge."

"Think he could have had anything to do with Sheldon's demise?"

She shook her head. "No. No way. Those two were as thick as thieves."

"Is there anyone else we should look into? What about Darius Creel?"

Talia groaned. "Now that guy is a real scumbag."

"How so?"

"He signed Sledge to a shitty deal, and he was always trying to screw him over. He owed us a ton of money. Sheldon was trying to get out of the contract."

"Maybe he didn't want Sheldon to leave," I suggested.

"Hell no, he didn't want him to leave. Sledge was his cash cow. He'd been taking all the publishing rights. Sheldon was fighting to get those back along with control of the master recordings. He wanted to start his own label. Who needs a record company anymore?"

"Amen," JD said.

"I'm assuming Sheldon's entire estate and his royalties will pass to you," I said.

She shrugged. "I guess. We're still married, after all. And we haven't updated our wills. I'll let the lawyers sort it out."

"Will you continue the lawsuit against the record label?"

"Absolutely. I'm not gonna let that sleazeball get away with this. Darius Creel has another thing coming if he thinks he can steal from me. This bitch don't back down!" she said with a sassy head shake.

"Has Darius ever threatened physical violence?"

She chuckled. "Shit. His whole business model is based on fear and intimidation. I don't think he ever directly threatened Sheldon, but he certainly tried to give the impression he was capable of bad things. I mean, that's how Sheldon got on his label in the first place."

"What do you mean?"

"Sheldon made the boneheaded mistake of signing an even worse deal with a label that wasn't going anywhere. I don't know exactly what happened, but the rumor is that Darius and his goons went over to the label's office and dunked the owner's head in a toilet bowl, plunging him underwater until he agreed to tear up the contract. Needless to say, he tore up the contract."

I glanced at JD.

"That wasn't the only time he did shit like that. I've got hundreds of stories about Darius Creel."

"Are you seeing anybody else currently?" I asked.

Her face twisted. "I don't see how that's any of your business."

"Just a question."

She paused, then relaxed. "Honestly, I decided to take a break. The last thing I need right now is to jump into another relationship. It wouldn't be fair to the other person. I'm not emotionally ready to commit, and nobody likes being a rebound."

"Anybody else we should look at?" I asked.

"Sheldon was always pissing off somebody."

"What about Kane Romo?"

Her face tensed. "I told him not to get involved with those losers." Her lips tightened, and she shook her head in frustration. "You think they could have done this?"

"Lucas says there was bad blood, but he didn't sound too concerned."

"It's stupid if you ask me. Sheldon knew what kind of people they were, yet he got involved anyway. Now that I think about it, Sheldon got himself in trouble every time he tried to help somebody out. What's the saying? No good deed goes unpunished."

"Something like that. I thought they were helping Sheldon out initially?"

"They were. But then Sheldon tried to help Kane with his *career*," she said in air quotes. "I tried to distance myself from that situation. I'm not really sure where things stood between Sheldon and Kane. But it wouldn't surprise me if they had a hand in this. We've been split for a few months, so I don't really know what was going on from day to day in Sheldon's life. I got all of my info from Lucas."

"So you kept in contact?"

She nodded. "I wasn't speaking with Sheldon directly. Lucas was acting as a go-between. I called him, and he would relay messages to Sheldon. Poor guy. I hated to put him in the middle, and I don't think he liked being there one bit."

I gave her my card and told her we'd be in touch. "Once again, my condolences for your loss."

She frowned. I think she was still dazed by the news.

Talia escorted us to the door, and JD and I ambled down the hallway toward the elevator.

"What do you think?" JD asked after Talia closed the door.

"I'll tell you after I confirm her alibi," I said.

"You don't think she actually gunned down her husband, do you?"

"No, but I'm not ruling out the possibility of her boyfriend trying to get Sheldon out of the picture."

"She said she doesn't have a boyfriend."

"People say a lot of things."

"You have trust issues."

I smiled. "That's why I'm still alive."

## 7

Darius Creel lived in the *Platinum Dunes Estates*. We cruised through the posh neighborhood, looking for his house. He had a sweet white Lamborghini in the circular drive.

We parked the Porsche at the curb and strolled the walkway to the front door. JD eyed the exotic sports car with a mix of envy and derision, though he'd never admit lusting after the Italian supercar.

I rang the video doorbell, and a minute later, Darius's smooth voice filtered through the speaker. He had a low radio DJ voice. "There's no soliciting in this neighborhood."

I flashed my badge to the camera. "Not selling."

"You got a warrant?"

"We're just here to talk."

"I know that game."

"Did you know that MC Sledge is dead?"

"What!?"

"He was murdered last night."

"I know you don't think I did it."

I smiled. "We thought you might have valuable information and insights. Sledge was your biggest star."

"You got that right."

"We'll just take a minute of your time."

Darius was silent for a moment. "Alright. Hang on."

The speaker crackled as it disconnected. We waited on the porch for a few minutes.

JD glanced around, taking in the sports car and the large estate with perfectly manicured hedgerows. "These guys are making bank. I mean, we did okay on the last couple of singles. But let me tell you, streaming revenue doesn't pay for something like this."

"Maybe you're making the wrong style of music," I teased.

JD's eyes narrowed at me. "It ain't about the money. I'm just saying. Maybe these guys are into more than just music."

Darius pulled open the door, and his suspicious eyes surveyed the two of us. He was a big guy at 6'5" with a beard and a close-cropped Mohawk. He wore a T-shirt, jeans, and expensive sneakers. He had a diamond pinky ring on his finger and gold chains dangling from his neck. "You two don't look like cops."

"We're a special crimes unit," JD said with a smile.

Darius squinted at him. "You're that guy…"

JD nodded. "Wild Fury."

Darius smiled. "I dig it. Old-school, with a new vibe. You got a label?"

"Don't need one."

"You say that, but look around. I've got connections."

"Different style of music."

"No doubt. But that gives me an idea. Maybe we can do a crossover. You guys could cut a single with one of my artists. Put it out on my label. No long-term contract. One song. What's the harm?"

"I'll keep that in mind," JD said.

"You guys must be something if Chloe-C had you open for her. She's the biggest pop star on the planet."

JD grinned. "We do have a little bit of mojo."

"Hey, my number one act ain't around anymore. I gotta start thinking about the future."

"Album sales usually skyrocket after an artist's death," I said.

Darius nodded. "They do. Then there are greatest hits compilations, unreleased tracks, remixes. Hell, there could be three or four posthumous MC Sledge albums."

"And you control all those rights," I said.

"I do. What's your point?"

"No point. Just making an observation."

"Sledge was the goose that laid the golden egg. Despite what you may think, I stood to make a lot more money if he was still around pumping out quality records."

"Not if he was pumping out quality records on his own label or if he won his lawsuit and took the rights to the original masters."

Darius tensed. "Okay. I see where this is going. Now I regret opening the door. Just when I was starting to like you two."

"You know the drill," I said. "These are just questions I gotta ask."

Darius frowned. "These are the kind of questions I don't like being asked. I'm just gonna put it to you straight. I didn't kill MC Sledge. Might be hard to believe, but I considered him a friend. Even if he was suing me."

"Maybe you have some thoughts about who might have killed him."

"Oh, I got some thoughts on that."

"I'm all ears," I said. "But let's get this out of the way first. Where were you last night?"

"I was in the studio, producing a new artist."

"Where's your studio?"

"Right here. No need for fancy studios anymore. I got everything I need in the comfort of my home—a great set of microphones, all the electronic processing equipment I need, state-of-the-art speakers, a nice mixing console. The room is soundproof, and I'm surrounded by luxury," he said with a smile, holding his arms out, displaying his property proudly.

"Very nice home you have."

"Thank you."

"Who's the new artist?"

"Jace Holiday. The kid's gonna be a household name. He's got a smooth, soulful voice, and the ladies love him."

"Let's hear your thoughts on who killed Sledge," I said.

"I need to have more details if I'm gonna come up with a theory."

I glanced at JD, then gave Darius limited details.

Darius shook his head. "That's a damn shame." He paused. "You know he was going through a pretty nasty divorce."

"His wife has an alibi."

"You verified that?"

"Yeah. I called the person she claims to have been with, Naomi Bowser. Her story checks out. And I doubt Talia showed up at the island and gunned Sledge down."

"I wouldn't put anything past that bitch."

"I take it you two didn't get along."

"Don't let her looks fool you. That woman is ruthless."

"Don't tell me you're afraid of her?" I said it just to egg him on.

His eyes narrowed at me. "Do I look like I'm afraid of anyone?"

I didn't imagine there were too many people that could intimidate Darius Creel.

"Tell me about their relationship?"

"What do you want to know? She was controlling, manipulative, and turned Sledge against me. I built Sledge up from nothing, then she came along and convinced him that I was out to screw him."

"From what I hear, the deal Sledge had with you was pretty onerous."

"It's a standard industry deal. No artist gets a great deal their first time around. It's part of the game. Do you know how much time, effort, and money I spend on artist development? 9 out of 10 times, the artist doesn't go anywhere. I gotta recoup those costs somehow."

"Maybe you should pick better artists," JD said.

Darius shot him a look. "Keep it up, and I'm gonna take my offer back." Darius addressed me. "Look, I was trying to work out a deal with Sledge. We were going to renegotiate the contract with more favorable terms. He was gonna drop the lawsuit. Now that he's dead, that's never gonna happen, and I gotta deal with that bitch. Do you think I'd knowingly put myself in that situation?"

If Darius was on the verge of a deal with Sledge, killing him seemed counterintuitive. But Darius could have been full of it.

"Who else had incentive to kill Sledge?"

## 8

"**I**f I was you, the first person I'd be looking for would be DJ Spinx," Darius said.

"Lucas mentioned him," I said.

"Yeah, that cat's out there. He ain't right in the head. I knew he was trouble from the minute I looked at him. Don't ask me what Sledge saw in him." He shook his head. "I mean, I get it. Sledge had a soft spot for these up-and-comers. But when I heard the demos they cut..." Darius cringed like he smelled something foul, "It was bad. Even with autotune, it was pitchy. I really don't know what Sledge was thinking."

"Spinx made threats?"

"He was livid when things didn't work out. He threatened me, threatened Sledge, threatened Lucas. I was like, *kid, you're messing with the wrong person.* You don't ever want to threaten me. If you want to cause me harm, you better just do it. Don't talk about it. Don't telegraph your intentions because I'll take you out first.'"

Darius liked to talk a big game, but he also looked like a guy that had the means to back it up.

"How did you handle the threats?"

"Shit... That little bastard came over here one day mouthing off, talking about how he was gonna blow up my house, fire-bomb my cars... I'm not gonna say what happened next, but I made it real clear that his mouth was writing checks his ass couldn't cash."

"What did you do?"

Darius smiled. "I don't recall."

"Smart answer," JD said.

"Mama didn't raise no dummy."

"What about Kane and the Dragon Nation?"

Darius shook his head. "Kane's a little punk bitch. Those guys are good at marketing their brand—badass gangsters. If you ask me, they're just wanna be hoodlums. I can't figure why anyone would go to those lengths to craft an outlaw image. I mean, Kane's loaded, to begin with. Bought Bitcoin back in the day when it was nothing. But money doesn't buy sense."

"I heard he was pretty pissed off about the deal going south."

"Sledge did him a favor. That kid raps worse than DJ Spinx. He didn't want those shitty tracks on the Internet. Sledge saved him a lot of embarrassment."

"Maybe that's not the way Kane sees it."

"I'm not gonna pretend that I know how another man sees the world." Darius paused. "Who knows? Kane felt slighted

—that much is certain. Maybe he felt forced to retaliate to save face."

"Anybody else you can think of?"

Darius hung his head, bit his lip, and thought for a moment. "You know, there is this one cat. He started making death threats on social media. Even sent a letter here once. I think I still got it. It was nonsense. We get a lot of kooks. He was mad and thought that Sledge was putting *subliminal* messages in his music, speaking directly to him. Said they were putting suicidal thoughts in his head, and he felt like Sledge was targeting him personally. Said if Sledge released another album, he would kill everybody responsible." Darius shook his head. "Ain't nothing subliminal in the music we put out. It actually bothered me because this guy needs help. He's out there with these wacky thoughts. He could do harm to himself or to the people around him. I wasn't worried about him going after any of us, but you never know. The messages on social media were posted from an anonymous account, and the letter didn't have a return address."

"When did the letter arrive?"

"Maybe a month ago. I forgot all about it."

"You still have the letter?"

Darius nodded. "Yeah. I stuffed it in a drawer. I don't know why. It just bothered me, and I thought, you know... I should keep this."

"Do you mind if we take a look at it?"

"Sure. I can get it for you."

"Did anyone else touch the letter besides yourself?"

Darius shook his head.

I pulled a pair of nitrile gloves from my pocket. "Mind if I grab the letter?"

"Sure. I'll show you where it is."

Darius stepped aside and allowed us to enter. "I know what you're gonna do. You're gonna take it to the lab and try to pull a latent fingerprint. Maybe get a DNA sample from the stamp or the sticky part of the envelope."

"You ever think about a career in law enforcement?" I joked.

He pondered the thought and smirked. "Detective Creel. I think I like the sound of that. I could solve some shit. I grew up on the streets. I know how these people think."

Darius's office was adjacent to the foyer which was massive and had a spiral staircase up to the second floor. He opened the door and motioned us in. There were several platinum albums and framed art on the walls, along with pictures of Darius with several of his artists holding more platinum records and music industry awards. He moved around the black desk and pulled open the drawer. He pointed to the letter. "There it is."

I snapped on the nitrile gloves, picked up the paper, and unfolded it. I read the letter. As Darius had described, it was somewhat incoherent and threatening, making outlandish claims and wild conspiracies. I figured it was either a joke or a seriously disturbed individual.

I sent JD to the car to grab an evidence bag. He returned, and I put the letter inside and sealed it. "I'll need Jace Holiday's information to verify your whereabouts."

"Sure thing." Darius texted the contact information to me.

I gave him my card and told him we'd be in touch. "Let me know if you think of anything else that might be helpful."

"I'll put my ear to the ground. See what the word is on the street. There will be lots of rumors and speculation about this. I also expect some people might try to take credit for it to pump their image. You might stumble across a lot of misinformation."

"I'll keep that in mind."

Darius escorted us out. He shut the door behind us as we strolled past the Lamborghini on our way to the Porsche.

I dialed Jace Holiday as I climbed into the car. JD cranked up the engine, and music pumped through the speakers. I turned the volume down so I could hear.

Jace answered the phone with a sharp tone. "Who's this? And why the fuck are you calling me?"

"I just spoke with Darius Creel. My name is Tyson Wild."

"Oh, I'm sorry. My bad. What you need?"

His tone changed, obviously thinking I was in the industry. I decided not to tell Jace I was a deputy. At least, not right away.

## 9

"Darius was telling me about the tracks you're working on," I said.

"Yeah, they're coming along great. We were just in the studio last night tracking vocals."

"Fantastic. I can't wait to hear them. What time were you in the studio last night?"

"We knocked it out pretty quick. I think we started at 10, and we were done by midnight."

"Impressive," I said.

"You work with Darius?"

"I manage Wild Fury," I said. It wasn't a lie.

"Right on. Those guys are old-school rock, right?"

"You got it."

He hesitated. "So, why you talking to me. I ain't looking for a manager, and I ain't your style."

"Darius mentioned the possibility of a crossover collaboration. I just thought I'd reach out and introduce myself. Who knows. This business is all about networking, right?"

"Ain't that the truth. I wouldn't be where I am today without contacts."

"Who introduced you to Darius?"

"MC Sledge."

"How do you know Sledge?"

"Shit, I used to sell him some weed. I just happened to mention I rapped. He heard my flows and introduced me to Darius. Darius signed me on the spot. Sledge takes a cut."

"Funny how the world works," I said. "Did Sledge buy a lot of weed?"

"Hell yes. He was my best customer. Of course, he wanted a discount for hooking me up with the label. So, it cut into my profit margin a little bit when I sold to him. Hopefully, I don't have to hustle that shit for too much longer. When this music thing blows up, I'm going legit. I won't need to mess with that nickel and dime crap."

"You ever sell Sledge anything else besides weed?"

"You know, a little of this, a little of that. What you need?"

"It's not for me, but the guys in the band have pretty big appetites. What have you got?"

"I can get coke, molly, meth, smack. All quality shit. Just let me know what you need."

"Where does your supply come from?"

"Trade secret."

"I just want to make sure it's coming from the right place."

"Oh, it comes from the right place. Shit is fresh off the boat. Never been stepped on."

"Good to know," I said. "I guess you haven't heard yet."

"Heard what?"

I told him Sledge was dead.

"No shit? What happened?"

I gave him limited details.

"That's terrible. Now you got me all depressed."

"Got any idea of who might have wanted him dead?"

Jace was quiet for a moment. "Shit, I don't know."

"If you hear anything, give me a call."

"Yeah, will do. Were you guys close?"

"You could say I've got an interest in finding out who killed him."

"What, did he owe you money or something?"

I chuckled. "No. Nothing like that. I'm just an interested party."

"Alright, bro. I'll keep in touch."

"Thanks. And good luck with the new tracks."

"Right on!"

I ended the call. Jace would figure out I was a cop when he talked to Darius. It sounded like he didn't know much, and I didn't want to get sidetracked chasing down a low-level dealer. But I figured it might be good leverage if we needed to lean on him in the future.

We drove back to the station, logged the evidence, and gave it to the lab. We stopped by Denise's desk to say hello. The office was buzzing with activity. Phones rang, and keyboards clacked. The stunning redhead was out of her luxurious evening gown and back into her uniform. Either way, she looked damn good.

She greeted us with a warm smile. "I'm working on getting phone records, and the lab is running ballistics on the slugs recovered from the site. We should know something soon. Are you guys making any progress?"

I shrugged.

She frowned.

"You want anything to eat?"

"Where are you going?" she asked.

I looked at JD.

"I'm thinking stuffed crab from Craig's Crab & Claw," Jack said.

Denise's eyes lit up. "Bring me shrimp tacos and a diet soda."

"Done," JD said.

We hadn't been to *Craig's Crab* in a long time. It was a typical party seafood joint. It was in the shape of an old white wooden boat. The inside was decorated with life preservers and fishing nets. There was an outdoor deck that overlooked the water and the dock. It was a great summer place when you were out on the water and wanted to zip in for a quick bite to eat. They served everything from boiled crawfish to po' boys. They had a good happy hour special and live bands in the evenings.

The hostess seated us outside, and a waitress attended to us shortly thereafter. Jack ordered his stuffed crabs, and I went for the Cajun chicken sandwich. From where I was sitting, I caught a glimpse of the flatscreen display behind the outdoor bar nestled in the shade under a Tiki hut.

Paris Delaney gave a breaking news report. "We are here at the courthouse where we're waiting to catch a glimpse of Mad Dog Whalen as he's transferred back to the county lockup. We're told that he has accepted a plea agreement for involuntary manslaughter, receiving a sentence of 10 years. His two bodyguards are currently under indictment as co-conspirators in the crime. I guess fans will be waiting a long time for another rematch between Mad Dog and Bobby the Butcher. For Action News, I'm Paris Delaney."

I was a little surprised that Mad Dog took the deal. I figured he'd fight it all the way. I wondered what life in prison would be like for the boxer. Would inmates constantly try to challenge him in an attempt to prove themselves? Or would they leave the giant be?

There was no doubt Mad Dog could handle his own.

We chowed down and took Denise's shrimp tacos to go. We dropped them off at the station, and she was most appreciative. I had her look up information for DJ Spinx, a.k.a. Charles Bradford. I made note of the address.

As we left the station, Paris Delaney accosted us in the parking lot. She had a cameraman and a sound guy in tow. The lens focused on us. The mic, shielded by a fluffy windscreen that looked like a dead cat, hovered on a boom pole overhead. "What can you tell me about MC Sledge's murder?"

Usually, I wouldn't mind getting accosted by a stunning blonde, but Paris Delaney could be a handful at times. Persistent and tenacious, an uncompromising reporter who would stop at nothing to get her story. Sometimes the exposure she provided was helpful, and sometimes it wasn't. I had a complex relationship with the beauty.

"We don't discuss ongoing investigations," I said.

Paris wouldn't be dismissed so easily. "Was this gang-related?"

"We don't know."

"Were drugs involved?"

I said nothing.

"Do you have any suspects?"

I smiled thinly. "We have promising leads."

We climbed into the Porsche, and JD cranked up the engine. We pulled away as the camera crew continued filming.

Paris stood in front of the lens and finished the segment with her trademark tag.

I had to admit, I was a little surprised she didn't show up at Starfish Key island during the initial investigation. She was a little slow getting her information this time. This was a high-profile case and would draw a lot of media attention. I had no doubt I hadn't heard the last from Paris Delaney.

"She's something, isn't she?" JD said.

"She is indeed."

"Maybe we should give her more information. I bet she could solve these things for us."

I chuckled. "I bet she could."

We cruised across town—the top down, the wind swirling, the Florida sun warming my skin.

Spinx lived in an eyesore on Bullhead Street. The shotgun shack was nestled in between two small but well-kept homes.

Spinx's place looked like it should have been condemned. The roof had seen better days, and the dingy white paint was peeling. The teal blue accents around the windows and door frames were faded. At first, I thought it was a fake address, picked at random from the Internet. The grass was overgrown, and the weeds were attempting to overtake the house.

We hopped out of the car and pushed through the chain-link gate. There was a low concrete wall that ran along the sidewalk that partitioned the front yard. Weeds growing through the crevices, and large sections of paint had flaked away, revealing the cinder block underneath.

The wooden boards creaked as we stepped onto the porch, and a no trespassing sign warned visitors to stay away. I banged on the door, not expecting an answer.

After a few more knocks, a low growl emanated from within. "Who is it?"

"Coconut County. We'd like to ask you a few questions."

There was a long silence.

I imagined the neighbors hated this place. It had to be dragging down property values.

DJ Spinx finally opened the door. "What do you want?"

Spinx looked like he had just woken up. His jeans hung low, revealing his red boxers. He had no shirt on and no shoes. He wiped the sleep from his eyes.

"When was the last time you saw MC Sledge?" I asked.

## 10

"I haven't seen Sledge in a long time," DJ Spinx said. "Only way I talk to him is through my lawyer."

"You're suing him for copyright infringement," I said.

"Yeah."

"How's that working out for you?" JD asked.

Spinx's eyes narrowed at him. "Fuck you. That cat stole my music, plain and simple. He's living over there on that private island of his, making bank on my royalties while I'm living in squalor."

"He's not living on the island anymore," I said.

Spinx's eyes rounded. "Oh really? Did he buy another island?"

"Not exactly. But he's got a new address."

Spinx shook his head in disgust. "Shit. I don't want to know." He hesitated for a moment. Then curiosity got the best of him. "Nice place?"

I shrugged. "Don't know. It could go either way."

Spinx's face crinkled, not sure what I meant.

"Where were you last night?" I asked.

His face soured. "Why do you want to know?

"Because somebody put a bunch of holes in MC Sledge."

Spinx's jaw dropped. "No shit? Sledge is dead?"

I nodded.

"Serves him right. I guess he finally screwed over the wrong person."

"Is that person you?"

"Oh, no! Don't look at me like that. I had nothing to do with nothing. I was working last night."

"Where do you work?"

He hesitated, then came clean. "I'm actually in between employment opportunities at the moment."

"So, where were you last night?"

"I was here. Working on rhymes. I got a ton of new material, and when I get enough money saved up, I'm going back into the studio. I'm going to record the tracks *my way* and put them out on my own label. They're gonna be hits, too. You watch."

"I'm sure."

"Don't patronize me."

"You own a gun?"

"No."

"Mind if we look around your place?" I knew what the answer was going to be before I asked.

"You got a warrant?"

"If you don't have anything to hide..."

"Man, don't give me that crap. I didn't do nothing."

"Seems like Sledge wasn't your favorite person," I said.

"Doesn't mean I killed him."

"But you made threats?"

"People say shit when they're pissed."

"This your house?"

"No. I'm fixing it up," Spinx said. "The owner lets me stay here in exchange. It's just temporary until I catch a break. Which is going to happen eminently."

"I heard you choked under pressure," I said.

Spinx's face crinkled. "What!? Where the hell did you hear that?"

"I heard you got in front of the mic and froze up." I was trying to get under his skin. "You stuttered, forgot the lines, sang out of tune."

The muscles in his jaw flexed, and his eyes blazed at me. He breathed heavily through his nostrils. He stammered, "I kn-kn-know what you're trying to do, and it ain't gonna work."

"I'm just trying to get to the truth."

"The truth is I didn't kill MC Sledge."

"You had motive, and you don't have an alibi," I said.

"Where was he shot?"

"On Starfish Key."

"Okay, *Mr. Smartypants*. Riddle me this... how did I get out there? Do you see a boat around here? Did you even bother to check registration records? I don't own a boat."

"Maybe you borrowed one."

He scoffed and shook his head. "I'm d-d-done talking to you."

He slammed the door in our faces. The window panes rattled, and for a moment. I thought the whole house might fall down.

We stepped off the porch and walked back to the car. When Jack slipped behind the wheel, he said, "Well, he's smarter than he looks. "

I called Denise and asked her to check the vessel and title registration records for good measure to see if anything was registered to Charles Bradford.

Her fingers clacked the keys. "Nope. Nothing."

"Ballistics come back yet?"

"Still waiting."

"Keep me posted," I said before ending the call.

We headed across town to find Lincoln Cross. According to the records, he lived on a boat in *Mangrove Bay*. We stopped in the office and spoke with the manager, Liberty. She eyed us with concern the moment we stepped through the door. Our investigations had taken us to *Mangrove Bay* a few times before.

"What is it now? Please don't tell me someone else died in the marina?"

I shook my head. "No. Not in the marina."

"Good grief," she groaned.

"We're looking for Lincoln Cross."

She frowned. "That poor man. I feel so sorry for him. I can't imagine what he's dealing with."

I lifted a curious eyebrow.

"Losing a child. So devastating."

"You mean Kayla?"

Liberty nodded. "I really shouldn't talk about other people's business, but..."

"What happened?"

She hesitated, glanced around, and whispered, "I don't want to speak out of turn. I'd just be repeating hearsay. Best you hear the story directly from him."

She gave us directions to Lincoln's boat.

We left the office and strolled down the dock, past the sailboats and yachts.

*Mangrove Bay* was a nice marina with a variety of watercraft —35-foot sailboats, sport-fishing boats, motor yachts, wake boats, houseboats, and the occasional superyacht.

We found Lincoln's boat—a 48-foot Valkyrie Sportfish. A damn nice boat. Sleek lines and tinted windows. *Kayla's Dream* was painted in script across the transom.

I banged on the stern and shouted, "Mr. Cross! Coconut County. We'd like to talk to you for a minute."

## 11

Lincoln Cross emerged from the salon and stood in the cockpit. He was in his early 40s, had brown hair, brown eyes, and tanned skin. He wore a T-shirt, board shorts, and deck shoes.

I flashed my badge.

"What can I do for you boys?"

"We'd like to talk to you about MC Sledge."

He smiled. "I just saw the news. Terrible tragedy."

"You seem real broken up about it," I said.

"The guy was a creep. I signed a nondisclosure agreement as part of the settlement, so I'm not supposed to talk bad about him. I guess it doesn't matter anymore." He smiled again. "What's he going to do? Sue me?"

"Out of curiosity, why did you and your daughter agree to settle?"

His face tensed, and his cheeks reddened. "Because I didn't want to put her through the ordeal. It was a nightmare as it was. You know what it's like for a 16-year-old girl to be thrust into the spotlight like that? The news media hounding you at every turn. The harassment she got at school. The things other kids said about her. The minute she got on the witness stand, a defense attorney would attempt to shred her character and make her out to be a liar. And in the end, what would she get out of it? I wanted to save her from the trauma. And I figured we could use the money towards college and maybe have a little left over to give her a nice start."

"Settling allows the alleged perpetrator to continue his pattern of abuse," I said, playing devil's advocate.

Lincoln didn't like the statement too much. Understandably so. His jaw tightened. "Not allegedly. He abused my daughter. I don't care what anyone says. I believe Kayla. She wouldn't lie about something like that."

"I understand she passed. I'm very sorry for your loss. Can you tell me exactly what happened?"

He took a deep breath, then let out an exasperated sigh. "I wish I knew exactly what happened." He swallowed hard, and his eyes brimmed. He took a moment to steady himself. "All she ever wanted to do was sing." His voice quivered, and his throat tightened.

A few tears spilled out of his eyes and dripped down his cheeks. He wiped them away quickly, sucked in a deep breath, and held tight.

He let the moment pass and muscled through it. "She had a beautiful voice. Like an angel. As a long shot, she sent videos of herself to Sledge. When he responded, we really believed this was her shot. I'm embarrassed I was so naïve. I thought for sure there was no way a guy like MC Sledge would take an interest in my daughter beyond her obvious talent. I had no idea he saw something else."

"So you didn't accompany her to the recording sessions?"

Lincoln glared at me. "No. And that is my biggest regret. I didn't want to encroach on her moment. I didn't want to make her feel self-conscious. I wanted her to do her thing. Kayla had always been very worldly and independent. I figured she could take care of herself. Everything seemed above board. Like I said, I was stupid not to think Sledge had ulterior motives."

He hung his head in shame.

We waited as he took a moment.

Lincoln took a breath and continued, "After the whole thing went down, Kayla went to live with her mother in Georgia. We both thought it would be a good idea for her to get into a new environment. Get away from this place."

He couldn't hold back any longer. The tears spilled over again.

Lincoln broke down into sobs, then recomposed himself before continuing. "She took a bottle of sleeping pills and never woke up. By the time they found her, it was too late." He shook his head. "She didn't even leave a note."

That twisted my stomach.

"She'd been through a traumatic experience, but I thought she was moving past it. We talked every couple of days, and she always sounded fine."

"I'm so sorry," I said.

"*Sorry* ain't gonna bring her back."

"Can you tell me where you were last night?"

His eyes blazed into me. "I was here on the boat."

"All night?"

"Yes. All night. And no, I didn't take my boat out to his island and gun him down, as much as I would have liked to."

"Do you own a gun?"

"A few of them."

"I don't suppose you'd let us take a look around your vessel?"

He stared at us with an incredulous gaze. "You guys are really gonna come around here and harass me after all I've been through?"

"It's standard procedure. You had motive, means, and opportunity. We'd just like to be able to cross you off the list and continue with our investigation."

"Why even bother? Who cares about a guy like Sledge? Whoever shot him did the world a favor. He can't hurt anybody anymore."

"We're just doing our jobs."

"Why didn't you do your job when my daughter was getting abused?"

"I believe there was an investigation at the time."

"Nothing came of it," he said, his face tense.

I paused. "I can call the Coast Guard. You're on the water. They can search the boat."

"I'm well aware of the law. If you want, take a look around. Be my guest."

We stepped aboard, and I glanced around the cockpit, looking for shell casings that may have found their way into the nooks and crannies. The vessel had a spacious 144-square foot cockpit with a 48-gallon bait tank at the stern and a big game door for getting those trophy fish aboard easily. Padded bolsters lined the gunwales, and there were multiple storage compartments.

Lincoln scowled at us with a hateful gaze as we searched the compartments.

"Mind if we look inside?" I asked.

"Do what you gotta do," he said.

## 12

W e stepped into the salon. With gorgeous woodwork, teak flooring, and comfortable leather seating, the interior was elegant and spacious. Ample lighting from large windows bathed the salon. A flatscreen display provided entertainment, and a full galley was outfitted with a stovetop, microwave, refrigerator, freezer, and stainless steel sink. A centerline staircase led to the below-deck quarters.

It reminded me of Jack's first sport-fish, the *Slick & Salty*, though slightly nicer. We searched the entire vessel, trying not to be too disruptive. We found a .45 ACP, a 9mm, and a 12-gauge pistol-grip tactical shotgun. The 9mm was of particular interest to me. We found it in a compartment in the master stateroom. "Mind if we take this to the lab and run ballistics?"

"I feel like I need an attorney," Lincoln said as I held the pistol in my gloved hand. He hovered just outside the hatch to the master stateroom.

"Why would you need an attorney?"

"So I don't get railroaded for something I didn't do."

"I've never seen a false positive on a ballistics test. It's like a fingerprint."

Lincoln threw his hands in the air. "Fine. I've got nothing to hide."

My thumb pressed the mag release button, and the magazine dropped into my palm.

It was full.

I placed it in an evidence bag, then ejected the round in the chamber and bagged it along with the pistol. "We'll get back to you in no time. We appreciate your cooperation."

Lincoln scowled at us as we stepped out of the master stateroom. He followed us back up to the salon.

"By the way, Mr. Cross," I said. "What do you do for a living?"

"I'm retired. I recently sold my house, bought the boat, and I'm going to spend the rest of my life doing exactly what I want. Life is short."

I couldn't argue with that.

We left the salon, crossed the cockpit, and stepped to the dock.

Lincoln glared at us as we walked away.

JD muttered, "I guess we know where that million-dollar settlement went. That's a damn nice boat."

"It is."

"Think he did it?"

"Motive, means, and opportunity. He's reeling from the death of his daughter, and he blames Sledge."

"If somebody took advantage of my daughter, I'd want to fill them full of lead."

We climbed into the Porsche and headed back to the station. I studied the weapon on the drive. "I'm not sure if this is the gun."

JD gave me a curious glance.

"Spray pattern at the crime scene," I said. "There were a lot of bullets."

"You think it was a fully automatic weapon?"

"Could be."

"Lincoln seems like a halfway intelligent guy," JD said. "If he did kill Sledge, I'm sure he got rid of the weapon. You'd have to be a moron to keep something like that around."

"Thank God for morons, right?"

JD shrugged. "If people used a little common sense, they might not be so quick to kill each other."

At the station, we logged the pistol into evidence, and Denise found us in the hallway. "I've got news for you guys. Ballistics came back on the slugs recovered from Sledge's body and the hull of his yacht. Looks like two different guns were used."

I lifted a curious eyebrow. "More than one shooter."

She nodded.

I exchanged a quick glance with JD.

"Maybe that's why so many bullets at the scene," JD said. "Maybe Lincoln had an accomplice?"

"There's something else. Daniels wants you two to get over to the *Seven Seas*. A girl was found dead in her hotel room."

"When did this happen?" I asked.

"Call just came in. Brenda is on her way over now."

"We're on it," I said.

JD and I rushed out of the station, hopped into the Porsche, and sped over to the luxury hotel.

The *Seven Seas* was the premier resort on the island. There were private suites, bungalows, a private beach, and a relaxing pool complete with bar, lounge chairs, sunshades, and a stunning array of scantily clad beauties with oiled skin and oversized sunglasses.

The red and blues of the patrol car flickered in the parking lot along with an ambulance. We pulled into a parking space, hopped out, and rushed into the opulent lobby. I flashed my badge to the concierge. In a discreet whisper, she said, "Room #321."

We rushed past the waterfall to the bank of elevators and pressed the call button. The bell rang, and the doors slid open. We stepped aboard the lift and rushed up to the third floor.

Mendoza and Robinson lingered in the hallway while Brenda and a forensics team evaluated the scene. Camera flashes spilled out of the suite.

As we reached the room, I asked Mendoza for the background information.

"This is kind of a crazy one."

Crazy was pretty normal in Coconut Key.

Mendoza continued, "So, get this. Maid is cleaning rooms. She hears a bang. She knocks on the door, but there's no answer. She puts her key into the slot, but it's dead-bolted from the inside. She leaves and gets Carl, the head of security." He pointed to Carl standing nearby, wearing a suit and tie with an acetate nameplate over his breast pocket. "Carl knocks on the door. No answer." He paused. "Well, I'll let him tell you..."

Carl stepped into the conversation. He was a tall guy, dark hair, mustache, mid 40s with a little bit of a belly. We had a few interactions in the past. Good guy. "After what the maid described to me, I was concerned, so we broke down the door."

The doorframe was mangled, and the wood had splintered.

"I stepped into the room and saw what had happened, then I backed out and protected the scene until Deputy Mendoza arrived," Carl said.

"Did you check for vitals?" I asked.

Carl shook his head. "There was no need. It was pretty obvious she was gone." He paused, then said in a grim tone, "I gotta warn you. It's not pretty in there."

"Where's the maid?" I asked.

Carl pointed to her cart down the hall. She was busy cleaning other rooms.

"Did she step inside the room?"

Carl shook his head.

"Here's the really weird thing," Mendoza said. "The girl has one prepaid credit card. She paid for the room in cash, and the ID in her purse doesn't match anyone in our system."

Dread twisted in my stomach. I had a bad feeling about this, and I didn't even want to step into that room. There was a part of me that felt like if I never walked into that room, I could pretend it didn't happen. But I was gonna have to face the grim reality sooner or later. "What's the girl's name?"

"ID says Piper Dixon."

I took a deep breath and peered down the foyer. One of the forensics guys motioned me in. JD followed behind me.

My heart sank when I saw the dead woman on the bed.

## 13

There were two things I knew for certain. The woman laying on the bed with the pistol in her hand was not Piper Dixon. It was Quinn Palmer. And Quinn Palmer would never kill herself. Not unless it was done in sacrifice to save someone else. This was not one of those situations. She was a good agent and had served her country faithfully.

I didn't like the scene from the moment I saw it. At first glance, it appeared as though Quinn had put the pistol to her head and squeezed the trigger, putting a small hole in her right temple and a rather large hole on the left side of her skull.

Carl was right. It wasn't pretty.

Blood spotted the comforter, the carpet, and the nearby wall. The tangy scent of gunpowder still lingered in the air. The pistol had a threaded barrel, and a suppressor was attached to the end. Contrary to popular belief, suppressors don't make guns whisper quiet. They knock off 30 to 40 dB, making a deafening bang sound more like a pop. They go a long way toward preserving your hearing in close-quarter combat. The constant hissing in the ears is something we all tend to suffer from after years of gunfire. It seems to grow louder every passing year.

My face was tight, and a mix of sorrow and rage swelled within me.

"You know her?" JD asked, reading my look.

I nodded discreetly. "Old colleague."

I hovered at the foot of the bed and surveyed the body carefully as Brenda examined the remains.

"There's no blood splatter on her hand," I said.

"I noticed that," Brenda replied. "The gun is at an awkward angle too. It wouldn't fall so neatly on her belly."

"Somebody placed it there," I said. "Let's dust for prints. Let's also dust the sliding glass doors and any other hard surface. Somebody else was in here."

"How did they get out?" JD asked.

I slipped on a pair of nitrile gloves, slid open the glass door, and stepped onto the balcony. The room overlooked the beach, and the teal waves crashed against the shore. The sunlight glimmered on the water, and a nice breeze swirled around. I glanced to my right, then my left. There was a gap between balconies. The railing was close enough to traverse between the two. A physically fit killer could have escaped from the balcony, climbing laterally or vertically.

I rushed back into the room, marched down the foyer, and into the hallway. I asked Carl, "Can you find out if anyone rented the adjacent rooms as well as the rooms above and below?"

"Sure thing." He clicked the talk button on his walkie-talkie and communicated with someone at the front desk.

I stepped back into the room and rummaged through the dresser drawers and closet. Quinn had a few articles of clothing, toiletries, cash, her fake ID, and a prepaid card along with a prepaid cell phone.

Carl called into the room. "Tyson..."

I rejoined him in the hallway.

He pointed to the room next door. "323 is occupied by an elderly couple. 421 is a young couple. I think they are newly-weds. Room 319," he said, pointing to the other neighboring suite, "is empty as well as 221."

I thanked him for the information and marched next door to 323. I banged on the door, and a woman shouted back shortly thereafter. "Who is it?"

I flashed my badge to the peephole and identified myself.

She pulled open the door. She was a cheery elderly woman with curly gray hair, blue eyes, and saggy jowls. "What seems to be the trouble?"

"Have you heard or seen anything suspicious in the last few hours?"

Her brow knitted together. "Suspicious like what?"

"A pop that may have sounded like a muffled gunshot."

Her eyes rounded and she observed the commotion in the hallway. "A gunshot?"

"A loud snap."

She thought about it for a moment. Her husband joined her at the door. He was a tall, gray-haired man with a slight hunch to his back. "Harold, did you hear anything like a gunshot?"

His face scrunched up. "I don't think so. Then again, my hearing ain't what it used to be," he said, tapping his right ear. A hearing aid was inserted in the canal.

"We just got back from lunch," the woman said.

"Do you recall seeing anyone come in or out of this room next door," I said, pointing to #321.

She exchanged a glance with Harold, and the two shook their heads.

I smiled and gave them my card. "If you can think of anything that might be helpful, please contact me."

"What happened?" the woman asked.

"There's been a death next door."

She gasped and placed her hand over her heart. "Oh, my God. Was it an accident, or are we talking murder?"

"There's no cause for alarm, ma'am."

She exchanged another glance with her husband, not buying my attempts to understate the situation.

"Well, I don't know how comfortable I feel staying in this hotel with someone getting murdered next door."

"I don't think you're in any danger, ma'am."

She exchanged another wary glance with Harold as I left. She closed the door, dead-bolted it, and put the security chain on. Something told me she was going to ask for a refund and would probably check out by the end of the day.

I walked back to Carl. "And you said #319 is empty?"

He nodded. "According to the guest register."

"Can you let me in the room?"

"I sure can." Carl fumbled for his master key, walked down the hall, and inserted it into the slot. The light flashed green, and he opened the door and held it for me. I stepped into the foyer, clicked on the light, and pushed into the room. I noticed a few things right away.

The two queen beds were both made, but the comforter on the bed near the balcony was rumpled as if someone had sat down and disturbed it slightly. There was a half-empty bottle of water on the desk. A quick glance in the minibar told me that a few snack items were missing.

"The maid refreshes the minibar after each guest, right?" I asked Carl.

He nodded. "And we provide two complimentary bottles of water each day."

I looked at the desk, and there was one unopened bottle remaining.

"Do me a favor. Can you find the maid and tell me if she's let anybody into this room today or yesterday?"

"Sure. I can also call the front desk. We've got a record of every time somebody swipes a key in the slot. Some might call it an invasion of privacy. But we know every time you enter and exit the room." He clicked his walkie-talkie and made another call to the front desk.

## 14

"Maid said she let a guy in early this morning. Said he forgot his keys," Carl said after speaking with her. "Hotel records show this room as vacant yesterday and today. The maid described the guy as tall, dark hair, mid 30s, athletic build with sunglasses and a baseball cap. He had on a T-shirt and cargo shorts. Looked like any other tourist."

"Let's get her with a sketch artist to see if they can come up with something to go on," I said.

"She's terrified she's gonna lose her job," Carl said.

"It could just be somebody who got his room number mixed up and thought he was locked out. Who knows?" I said. "But it's the best lead we've got right now."

I had the forensics guys collect the half-empty bottle of water and dust the area for prints. Mendoza and Robinson canvassed the rest of the neighboring units to see if anyone had seen a man scale the balcony.

"Can you have the manager include a note with every customer's bill asking if anyone saw anything to contact Coconut County?"

Carl nodded. "I don't think management's gonna like broadcasting the fact that there was another death in the hotel."

"See what you can do."

Carl nodded.

I spoke with the maid in the hallway briefly, confirming everything Carl had relayed to me. Her name was Maria Torres.

I couldn't give her any assurances about her job security. It was not up to me. It was an honest mistake and something that happens all the time.

She shifted nervously as we spoke and looked like she was on the verge of tears. Her concern was compounded when the medical examiner rolled Quinn's body out of the unit on a gurney, zipped up in a body bag.

It felt like a punch to the gut. I needed to know who killed Quinn and why.

I finished speaking with Maria, and she went back to work.

JD whispered, "Quinn must have come into town late last night. Somebody followed her." He paused. "What the hell was she into?"

"I'm gonna find out," I said as I dialed Isabella's number.

She was my handler at *Cobra Company*. The clandestine agency did the dirty little jobs nobody else wanted to do or could do. They offered plausible deniability to the powers that be.

"We have a situation," I said.

"What is it now?" Isabella asked.

"Quinn Palmer is dead."

Isabella was silent for a moment. "How?"

I filled her in on the details.

"Was she working for you?" I asked.

"You know I don't discuss the status of operatives."

It was a frustrating answer, but not unexpected. "Who would want her dead?"

"Lots of people."

"Do you have a shortlist?"

"Not at the moment. But you can bet I'll come up with one."

"She was clearly targeted for assassination. Do you know what else she was doing outside of Cobra?"

"She was living in Miami with her boyfriend, picking up freelance work. Corporate security, dignitary protection, that kind of thing. She would track down the occasional missing person."

"Do you know if she was involved in anything shady?"

"You know as well as I do that's not Quinn's style. Sometimes people get in a bind, and they do things they normally wouldn't do for money, but there's nothing in her background to indicate she was compromised by finances."

"What about her boyfriend, William?"

"He was a securities analyst at an investment firm," Isabella said.

"I think he was an incidental target."

"I'll see what I can find out," Isabella gave a solemn pause. "I know you and Quinn go way back. This is as personal to you as it is to me."

"Absolutely."

"Find out who killed her and take care of it, and I'll be the one owing you favors."

"I'll take that deal."

"I figured you would. Pursue it through to a conclusion, wherever it leads. Nobody kills one of my operatives and gets away with it. We'll talk soon."

She ended the call, and I slipped the phone back into my pocket.

We wrapped up and headed down to the lobby. Mendoza and Robinson had talked to a number of guests, but no one recalled seeing a man scale the balcony. I figured it was the only way someone could enter and exit the room, leaving the deadbolt latched from the inside. Not unless somebody had the ability to walk through walls. But things hadn't gotten *that* weird in Coconut Key yet.

It shouldn't have surprised me to see Paris Delaney in the parking lot with her news crew. She swooped in like a vulture, the camera rolling. "Deputy Wild, what can you tell us about the deceased?"

I clenched my jaw. "I can't release any information at this time."

"Have you been able to confirm the identity of the woman?"

"No comment."

"Was this a suicide?"

My eyes blazed into her. "As I said, Ms. Delaney, I can't answer any questions at this time."

We pushed past her entourage, and she gave me a sassy frown.

We climbed into Jack's Porsche, and he cranked up the engine.

Paris stood in front of the camera and did a *stand and deliver* in front of the hotel, the emergency vehicles flashing in the background. I'm sure she got footage of the medical examiner removing Quinn's body.

"How the hell does she get these details?" JD asked.

"Hotel staff," I suggested. "Leak in the department."

Jack pulled out of the lot, and we headed back to the station to fill out after-action reports.

I called the Miami PD Homicide Division and spoke with Detective Curran. I identified myself as a deputy with Coconut County. "What can you tell me about the death of William Oliver?"

"Is there a number where I can reach you at?"

"This is my cell number. You can call me here."

"I'll need a departmental number," Curran said.

I understood his skepticism. I could have been anybody calling for information. I gave him the number to the sheriff's office—a number that was easily verifiable. He said he'd call me back in a few minutes. When he did, I had the call routed to Denise's desk.

"Deputy Wild?"

"Thanks for calling me back."

"I apologize for the precautions," Curran said. "It's just a weird case."

"How so?"

## 15

"The guy hung himself in his house," Detective Curran said. "No note. No history of depression. I talked to neighbors and co-workers. The guy had everything going for him. More money in the bank than I'll make in a lifetime. Doesn't make sense. And the live-in girl-friend is missing."

"She's not missing anymore," I said. "His girlfriend, Quinn Palmer, is dead."

I caught him up to speed, leaving out the part that Quinn was a clandestine operative. I continued to press him about William's death.

"Were there any signs of forced entry?" I asked.

"No."

"Did the neighbors see anything suspicious?"

"No."

"What does your medical examiner say?"

"The official report hasn't come back yet," he said. "And you're sure Quinn Palmer didn't kill herself?"

"Positive. I knew Quinn well. The way the gun was staged, and the lack of blood splatter on her hand indicates the weapon was placed after her death. I think you're gonna find that William Oliver didn't hang himself either. He was most likely strangled."

Detective Curran groaned. "It would take a pretty big guy to hoist him into the air."

"Or an accomplice."

"You got any leads on who is behind this?" Curran asked.

"Unfortunately, no."

Curran sighed in frustration. It was a complex case—one that could drag on and possibly never get resolved. "I'm more than happy to share information with you if you'll do the same with me."

"You got yourself a deal."

"Good luck," he said.

"You too."

I thanked him for his cooperation and hung up.

JD and Denise stared at me with curious eyes. I relayed the information.

"That's creepy," Denise said. "So, there's an assassin running around Coconut Key?"

"Whoever did this is trying to cover their tracks and not doing a very good job of it," JD said.

"The killer is probably long gone," I said. "This was just a distraction to slow law enforcement down." I paused. "If it were me, I'd bring someone in from out of town. Have them do the job and get out. Case grows cold and gets forgotten about."

"I know you're not going to forget about this one," JD said.

"Who was she?" Denise asked. "I mean, I know she was your friend. But how did you know her?"

"That's a story for another time," I said.

Denise rolled her eyes. "You boys and your secrets."

I smirked and shrugged innocently. "Hey, do me a favor. Look up Quinn's sister, Caroline Palmer, in Chicago.

Denise's fingers streaked across the keyboard. A moment later, Caroline's picture popped up on the screen along with her information.

"Yep, that's her." I made a note of her phone number and entered it into my contact list.

"So, did you date Quinn?"

"Why do you ask?"

Her eyes narrowed at me. "I'll take that as a yes."

"I didn't answer yet."

"I'm sorry, perhaps I phrased that incorrectly. Did you hook up with her?"

"Someone's jealous."

She scoffed. "I am not jealous. Curious. You should learn the difference."

I sneered at her playfully. She was a tad jealous.

"Get a room, you two," JD muttered.

"He wishes," Denise snarked.

No argument there.

JD looked at his watch. "I gotta get to band practice. You want to tag along?"

"Why not?"

I told Denise we would catch her later. She wiggled her manicured fingers at me as we left the office.

The deputy at the front desk called to me as we passed. "Deputy Wild, can you talk to this gentleman?"

"What seems to be the trouble?"

"I got robbed!" the man shouted. "That's what the problem is. And I want you to do something about it."

He was bubbling over with anger, and that anger was focused toward the department. It was understandable. People get frustrated, and the system can sometimes seem unresponsive.

"Tell me what happened?"

"I was on my boat with a friend. We weren't too far from Crystal Key. That's when the Coast Guard pulled up on us. At least, I thought they were the Coast Guard."

He had my full attention.

"Anyway, they boarded the boat, shoved their guns in my face, and took my stuff."

"What did they take?"

"Stuff."

"I need an itemized list."

"What good is that going to do?"

"If the items turn up in a pawnshop, maybe you can get them back."

"They took cash."

"How much cash?"

He shifted uncomfortably.

"If you don't talk to me, I can't help you," I said.

"$250,000. Cash money."

I lifted a curious brow. "$250,000?"

"Damn right, and I want it back!"

I was starting to see where this was going. "What were you doing on the water with $250,000?"

I knew what he was doing, but I asked anyway.

He shrugged. "I like to be prepared."

"Prepared for what?"

"In case I get a wild hair and decide to cruise around the globe at a moment's notice."

It was a load of bullshit.

"What kind of boat do you have?"

"A 35-foot speedboat."

"Yeah, you're definitely going to cruise around the globe on that," I said dryly.

He shrugged. "You never know."

"What were you doing out there?"

"Fishing."

More bullshit.

"So you were out on the water with $250,000, just walking around money, when you were ambushed?"

"Yeah."

The guy was clearly out there to make a drug deal. The pirates either attacked before or after the exchange. I wasn't sure which, and it didn't really matter. "How many were there?"

"Four guys."

"In a Coast Guard patrol boat?"

"They were decked out in tactical gear and had assault rifles. I thought we were busted at first," his eyes widened as he said it, realizing his slip.

"Did you get a look at their faces?"

"Nope. They all wore face coverings and helmets."

"When did this happen?"

"About an hour ago. A little over. I wasn't about to call the Coast Guard after that. I came back to the marina and drove straight here to report the incident."

"Maybe you ought to stop running around with so much cash on hand," I said.

His face crinkled. "That's your response? You ain't gonna do nothing? I'm an upstanding member of the community. I pay my taxes."

I doubted this guy paid taxes on his drug profits. "Tell you what. The next time you go out on the water with $250,000 in cash, call me. I'll give you a personal escort."

His face crinkled with curiosity. "Really?"

"Absolutely. We would hate to see such a fine citizen such as yourself experience another tragic loss."

I'd be more than happy to escort him to the next drug deal and bust him and his supplier.

He thought about it for a second. "I'll keep that in mind. What about my 250K?"

I shrugged. "We'll keep an eye out for it."

He shook his head. "Shit, you find that kind of cash you'd be a fool not to keep it."

"Your cash is gone. But believe me, I have every intention of tracking down the guys who robbed you. They robbed me too."

"No shit?"

I nodded. "Why don't you give me your name and number, and we'll keep in touch."

He thought about it for a moment. "Okay. I can do that."

The guy wasn't too bright.

The deputy at the front desk handed him a pen, and he scribbled his name and number on a piece of paper and handed it to me. His name was Harrison.

"You find my money, you call me," he said before leaving.

I smiled. "You got it."

"Sounds like our pirates are changing their MO," JD said.

"They're taking on a lot more risk robbing drug dealers. Those people shoot back."

"More risk, more reward."

I shrugged. "They were doing pretty good sticking to luxury yachts. Greed will catch up with you." I smiled. "And I hope to be there when it happens."

We left the station and walked across the parking lot to the Porsche. I called Quinn's sister and gave her the bad news. First, there was the initial shock. Then the sobbing. Then the cries of agony.

I tried to comfort her as best I could. I always hated making these phone calls.

When Caroline finally pulled herself together, she sniffled and asked, "Does this have anything to do with her line of work?"

"It's hard to say for sure right now, but that's a good bet."

"She was always cagey about what she actually did." She sounded stuffy from crying. "She would never really answer my questions, and eventually, I stopped asking."

"Did she express any concerns to you lately?"

"No. I haven't really talked to her all that much. We'd speak every few weeks and send messages here and there on social media. I feel bad that I didn't make more time for her. I've got my hands full with these two kiddos. The days just seem to slip away. This single mom thing ain't easy."

Caroline sniffled again.

"How well did you know William?"

"I liked him. He was good for her. Such a nice guy. He sure did love Quinn. I mean, who didn't, right? She had that personality. That smile." She gave a thoughtful pause. "She sure could light up a room."

"That she could," I said.

We were silent a moment as we remembered Quinn.

"Was William into anything of concern?" I asked.

"You know Quinn. She always kept her cards close to her chest. She never talked about personal stuff. Everything was always great—even if it wasn't."

It was just like Quinn to put on a good face no matter the situation. It made hearing her panicked voice when she called all the more concerning.

I assured Caroline that I would do everything in my power to bring Quinn's and William's killer to justice. I told her to call me if she could think of anything that might be helpful and expressed my condolences again before ending the call.

We headed over to JD's practice studio in the warehouse district. The sound of a band rehearsing filtered out of the building and echoed across the parking lot as JD pulled into a space near the entrance. The snap of a snare drum bounced off the neighboring buildings.

We hopped out of the car and strolled past the usual band of miscreants loitering around the entrance, smoking cigarettes. One of them high-fived JD. His long black hair fell into his eyes that were lined with mascara. They were a little glassy from indulging in some illicit substances. He was decked out in black jeans, black boots, a concert T, and studded bracelets. "Dude, caught a bootleg of the show in New York. Righteous stuff!"

JD gave him a quizzical look. "Where did you see it?"

"It's all over the Internet, bro."

A prideful grin curled on JD's face, and his chest puffed out. "Rock 'n' roll!"

We pushed inside and strolled down the dim hallway. Rehearsal spaces lined either side of the corridor, and music seeped out, along with the sweet herbal scent of weed.

We pushed into the practice studio, and Styxx was behind his candy-apple red drum set, tapping out a rhythm on the snare drum while Dizzy tuned his guitar.

Crash still had a cast on his arm. It had been replaced after we hacked away part of it in New York City to give him better access to the neck and fretboard of his instrument. He paid the price with some nasty swelling after the shows in

New York, and the doctor told him not to do that again. He was under strict orders not to play until his arm was fully healed and the cast removed.

Faye was still sitting in, despite what had happened in New York. She promised she was on the straight and narrow.

I took it with a grain of salt.

But she was showing up for practice and making all the gigs. She was a hell of a bass player—there was no doubt about it.

Crash had become quite taken with her. They had an unofficial *thing* going on, which created a little awkward tension in the band. As manager—and I use the term loosely (how do you actually manage the unmanageable?)—I had to maintain a forward outlook and prepare for possible bumps in the road. I wasn't really sure how the whole Faye scenario would play out long term.

Crash would get his cast off in a couple weeks and would be back in business. Faye would go back to her full-time gig with *Lip Bomb*. The band had a couple gigs lined up at *Sonic Temple* in the interim. They weren't monumental events like Madison Square Garden. But still, I didn't want to see the band implode or have to cancel shows due to interpersonal strife. Both JD and Crash had broken the band rules (set by JD) and had *encounters* with Faye.

It was understandable.

With her blonde pixie-cut hair, petite body, and alluring features, Faye was the epitome of the sexy rock 'n' roll icon. She had all the makings of a star and the requisite element of danger. That *life on the edge* quality that many rock and rollers seem to have. Like a freight train speeding toward a cliff. You couldn't help but watch and get caught up in the drama. Some of the biggest stars are always on the verge of self-destruction, enthralling the world with their delicate balance between life and death, like a performer on a high wire.

The scenario had the potential to go all kinds of wrong.

"Did you hear about the video?" JD asked the guys.

"The bootleg?" Styxx asked.

JD nodded.

"30 million views already," Styxx said with a smile.

The reviews after their show with Chloe-C had been over-whelmingly positive. It was a surprising turn after the band had received an avalanche of negative press after their first music video, despite it being a hit with the public. It seemed like the press was finally catching on to what the fans already knew. *Wild Fury* was a hard-hitting rock 'n' roll band that took no prisoners. The guys were willing to bleed for their art, and that was something you just couldn't fake.

The band ran through their setlist, and a wall of sound thundered from powerful amps. As usual, people started to filter into the practice studio for a free show.

Time with the band was always an opportunity to escape reality for a brief moment.

After practice, we all headed to *Tide Pool* for the obligatory after-party. JD bought a round for everyone, and Faye promised to exercise moderation. We hung out by the outdoor pool, watching the pretty people frolic in the water.

Music pumped through the outdoor speakers, and the scent of piña coladas and fresh chlorine swirled in the air.

There were plenty of visual delights to keep me distracted as bikini-clad beauties sauntered about, wet fabric clinging to pert assets. But my mind was somewhere else, thinking about Quinn and who would want her dead. Had she gotten into something she shouldn't have? Did she make a new enemy? Or was this something from her past?

In our line of work, you could never really stop looking over your shoulder.

## 16

I was cooking breakfast the next morning when Teagan appeared on the aft deck. The teal-eyed beauty cradled Fluffy in her arms and held onto Buddy's leash. The little Jack Russell wagged his tail excitedly.

I moved across the salon and opened the sliding glass door. Buddy rushed inside and put his paws on me, begging for attention. I knelt down and petted him and scratched his chin.

Teagan stepped into the salon and slid the door shut behind her. She let Fluffy down on the deck, and the aloof white cat strolled away and climbed onto the settee, resuming her throne.

"Thanks for taking care of these guys," I said as I stood up.

"My pleasure." She pouted. "I thought I'd drop them off before I start my shift. I almost don't want to give them back."

"You want breakfast?"

"No, thank you. Duty calls," she said, motioning to *Diver Down.* "But I'll take a raincheck."

I smiled. "You got it."

Teagan left, and I finished breakfast.

Denise called not long after. "We got a hit on the fingerprint pulled from that letter sent to Darius Creel."

I lifted an impressed brow. "Do tell."

"It belongs to a guy named Arlo Godfrey III. Heir to the Godfrey fortune. The guy is loaded. He has a prior arrest for stalking and online harassment. He was acquitted of both charges."

"Interesting."

"Daniels got a warrant for his arrest. When do you want to take him down?"

"Right now."

"I'll text you Arlo's address," Denise said. "He lives at *Fulmar Plaza*. I'll have Erickson and Faulkner meet you there in half an hour."

"Perfect."

"Oh, and the ballistics from Lincoln Cross's gun don't match the bullets found at the crime scene."

I frowned. "I'm not ruling him out just yet."

"I'll keep you posted."

"Thanks."

I ended the call, dialed JD, and filled him in. He swung by the marina and picked me up, and we headed over to Arlo's condo. The *Fulmar* was an upscale high-rise on the west side. There was an attached marina and a ton of amenities —weight room, sauna, tennis courts, indoor basketball courts, 24-hour concierge service, and valet parking. The building was older than the *Trident Towers* and a little more expensive—though, honestly, the Trident was nicer.

We pulled under the awning, and the valet grabbed JD's door. He flashed his badge and told the attendant to keep it upfront.

"Yes, sir," the attendant replied as he handed JD a ticket.

We waited for the other deputies to arrive. Their patrol car pulled into the lot a few minutes later and parked under the awning near the main entrance. The valet wasn't touching the patrol car.

"This guy is a lunatic," Erickson said. "We arrested him before. I think all that money screwed him up good."

Faulkner grabbed a battering ram from the trunk.

The doorman surveyed us with concern. He grabbed the door and held it as we strolled into the lobby.

The concierge's eyes grew round. She sprang from her desk and greeted us. "Is there some kind of problem?"

"No problem," I said with a grin. "Just executing an arrest warrant."

She eyed the battering ram with curiosity and concern. "You're not going to break down a door, are you?"

"If need be."

"Let me speak with the manager. I can probably provide access with a warrant."

I showed her the document.

She read the name. "Arlo? What did he do?"

"He made threats."

Her face crinkled. "He's a little odd, but do you think he's really dangerous?"

"We take all threats seriously."

She scampered away, consulted with the manager, then returned with a master key. We crossed to the elevators, and Jack pressed the call button. A moment later, the bell dinged, and the doors slid open. The team stepped aboard, and we launched to the 26th floor.

Arlo lived in a penthouse suite.

The concierge looked uncomfortable. "He's not like a terrorist, is he?"

"No, ma'am."

She seemed relieved. "Who did he threaten?"

"I can't discuss specifics."

We stepped off the lift, walked down the hall, and banged on 2602. After a few moments, a whiny, nasally voice shouted through the door. "Who is it?"

"Coconut County!" I said.

The concierge hung back and watched the show.

Arlo pulled open the door and stared at us with a perturbed face. He had curly dark hair, squinty brown eyes, and stood about 5'6". He was in his mid 30s and didn't seem too pleased to have visitors. "Why are you harassing me?"

"We're not harassing you. We're arresting you," JD said.

Arlo shot him a confused look. "Whatever it is, I didn't do it."

"Put your hands against the wall and spread 'em," I commanded.

His face crinkled, then he tried to slam the door. I put my shoulder into it before he could get it closed. He pushed back against the door, and I pushed it open, knocking him to the ground.

Arlo scampered to his feet and took off running down the foyer toward the living room.

I chased after him.

The vaulted living room had massive floor-to-ceiling windows, and a staircase led up to the second floor. The place was decked out with trendy leather furniture and massive canvases of fine art.

I caught up with him at about the time he hit the staircase. I grabbed the back of his shirt collar and yanked him down. Arlo tumbled back, but I held onto his shirt, keeping him from smacking his head against the tile.

JD pounced on him and slapped the cuffs around his wrists. He yanked the little perp to his feet.

Arlo groaned. "What the hell are you arresting me for?"

"You sent a letter to Darius Creel making threatening statements," I said. "A second-degree felony."

His face crinkled. "Who?"

"Darius Creel. He owns the record label that MC Sledge is signed to. *Was* signed to."

"I didn't threaten anybody," Arlo protested.

"Is that so?" I said, my voice drenched with sarcasm.

"You have the right to remain silent," JD said.

"The cuffs are really tight. They're cutting into my wrists."

"Life's a bitch," JD said, handing him over to the deputies.

They escorted him out of the building while we searched the condo. We confiscated his laptop and his printer. But we didn't find any weapons. If he made good on his threats against MC Sledge, he'd gotten rid of the murder weapons. But somehow, I just couldn't see Arlo double fisting two 9mm pistols, unloading both magazines into the rap star. But a guy like Arlo could afford to hire a hitman, or two, or three.

rlo sat under the fluorescent lights in the interrogation room wearing an orange jumpsuit, his hands cuffed.

He had been processed and printed, and we let him simmer in the tiny claustrophobic room for about an hour. JD and I pushed inside, and I dropped the letter onto the desk in front of him. It was sealed in a plastic evidence bag.

"Recognize that?" I asked.

Arlo didn't even look at it. "Nope."

"That's funny. Your fingerprints are on it."

"So?"

"You can't go around sending threatening letters to people, harassing them from anonymous accounts on social media. And you can't shoot rap stars."

His eyes rounded, and his brow lifted. "What!?"

"Oh, did I forget to mention...? MC Sledge is dead."

"Really?" He asked, not disappointed.

"Really."

He thought about it for a moment. "Well, I didn't kill him."

"Then why did you write a threatening letter to the owner of his record label?"

"I told you, I didn't write the letter. Just because you claim my fingerprints are on the paper doesn't mean I wrote the letter."

"You really want to play this game? Because you're gonna lose. We confiscated the printer at your house. Something tells me it's gonna match up with the inkjet nozzle pattern on this letter. But I guess you're gonna say that someone broke into your condo, wrote the letter on your computer, and printed it out on your machine, right?"

"Building security isn't what it used to be," Arlo muttered, deadpan.

"Who did you pay to kill MC Sledge?" I asked.

His face crinkled. "I didn't pay anybody to kill Sledge."

"So, you did it yourself?"

"No! What's with you people?"

"Hey, you're the one who sent the record label a letter threatening to kill him if he released another album because the voices were talking to you."

"Go ahead, laugh at me. But he was putting subliminal messages in the songs. Messages that could cause people to do dangerous things. He had to be stopped."

"So you stopped him?"

"No. But somebody did. God works in mysterious ways."

"I don't think God had anything to do with this."

"Of course he did."

"You and I have very different ideas about God. Where were you Friday night?"

Arlo hesitated. "I was at home, watching TV and listening to music."

"Did the voices tell you to kill Sledge?" JD muttered.

Arlo glared at him. "I wouldn't expect you to understand."

"By all means, please help me understand," JD said.

"Do you have any proof of any of these allegations?" Arlo asked.

I pointed to the letter. "What's that?"

"Writing a letter and killing someone are two different things," Arlo said.

"Are you admitting you wrote the letter?"

"I'm not admitting anything."

"You're looking at up to 15 years just for the letter."

Arlo swallowed hard.

"How about you start cooperating?"

"I've been cooperating."

I scoffed.

"I think I want an attorney."

It was a phrase that a lot of people said, thinking it would end the questioning. The phrasing stopped short of making an actual statement requesting an attorney. Never say *I think*... say *I want*—a subtle but important distinction.

"Do you have anyone that can verify your whereabouts Friday night?"

"Check my phone records. That will tell you my exact location."

"You could have left your phone at home. You've got a boat, right?"

"Two, actually."

"I know. I checked the registration—a sailboat and a racing boat. You could have taken the racing boat to Starfish Key island, gunned down MC Sledge, and gotten back to Coconut Key in no time."

He scoffed. "That's preposterous. I don't own a gun. I've never fired a gun in my life."

"So tell me who you paid to kill Sledge?"

"I told you, I want an attorney."

He finally said the magic words.

"Okay. Suit yourself."

I grabbed the evidence from the table and moved to the door. After a quick knock, a deputy buzzed us out, and we left Arlo in the interrogation room. The door closed with a clunk behind us.

"What do you make of that guy?" JD asked.

"I don't know. The way that guy's mind works only makes sense to him. We need to sift through his phone records, bank transactions, and anything else that might indicate he hired someone to take out Sledge. Either way, he's going to do time for the threats."

"Don't count on it," JD said. "Money buys a lot of influence, especially in this town."

I cringed, but JD was right. Coconut Key had its fair share of corruption. It seemed like we were battling against it at every turn. And a guy like Arlo had enough money to grease all the right palms.

Denise found us in the hallway. "Brenda was able to recover DNA from that water bottle you found in the hotel room next to Quinn's."

"And?"

## 18

"The DNA doesn't match anything in the criminal database," Denise said. "Quinn's killer doesn't have a serious record."

I frowned.

"Sorry." She nodded to the interrogation room. "You get anything out of this guy?"

"Not really."

"I know you have resources, but I'll put in a request for Arlo's phone records. Also, I tracked down Kane Romo. He's living on a yacht in Pelican Point. The name of the boat is *Scrilla*."

It was a slang term for money.

I thanked Denise for the info, and JD and I headed over to *Pelican Point*. We cruised across the island, the golden sun beaming down, wind swirling about the cabin. It was a gorgeous day.

We pulled into the parking lot and strolled the dock, looking for Kane's superyacht. It wasn't hard to find. It stuck out like a sore thumb.

Kane Romo was all about the *bling*. His 130' *Abiati Ventro* was a thing of beauty. It was too bad he had poor taste. The superyacht was lined with gold trim, and the name-board on the garage was encrusted with diamonds and adorned with money symbols. The gaudy yacht screamed for attention.

It always amazed me how criminals loved to paint targets on themselves. They were obsessed with outward appearances —more money equals more toys equals more power.

We stood on the dock, marveling at the ostentatious display of wealth. Scantily clad beauties sunned themselves on the foredeck. Pop music blasted through speakers, echoing across the water.

We crossed the passerelle to the aft deck and banged on the sliding glass door to the salon. The interior had an open floor plan with a dark hardwood deck, stylish modern furniture, and gold accents everywhere.

Nobody could hear us knocking, but there was a security camera on the aft deck.

We banged on the glass a few more times. A moment later, a scantily clad brunette in a skimpy bikini sauntered across the salon and slid open the door. She looked at us with an annoyed, snooty glance. "Can I help you?"

"We're looking for Kane," I said. "Is he around?"

"Who's asking?"

I smiled. "I'm Tyson, and this is JD."

Her eyes flicked between the two of us. "Is that supposed to mean something to me?"

A big, brawny dude emerged from a corridor in the salon behind her. The muscle-bound guy had short hair, a square face, and a thick neck. He wore dark sunglasses, a T-shirt, and cargo shorts. "What's going on?"

"Two assholes are here to see Kane," the girl said.

The muscle-bound guy said, "I'll handle it from here."

The brunette spun around and sauntered back to the fore-deck. She had a nice saunter. Her hips swayed from side to side, jiggling hypnotically.

"What's your business with Kane?" the muscle-head asked.

"We just want to ask him a few questions." I flashed my badge.

The big guy's face tensed. "Kane doesn't talk to cops."

"I don't blame him," I said. "Usually, I would say that's the smart thing to do. But not in this situation."

His face twisted. "Why is this situation different?"

It wasn't. But I hoped that maybe I could pique Kane's curiosity. Curiosity could often be a suspect's undoing.

"This might be Kane's only opportunity," I said.

"Opportunity to do what?"

"To clear his name."

The goon stared at us for a long moment. The muscles in his jaw flexed. "Kane doesn't need to clear his name of anything."

"Then he shouldn't be afraid to talk to us."

He hesitated a long moment, surveying us. "Hang on a minute."

He spun around and marched forward, disappearing down a passageway.

JD whispered, "Think Kane will talk? Or will they kick us off the boat?"

I thought for a second. "He'll talk. He's the smug, overconfident type."

"$100?"

"You're on."

We shook hands on the bet.

## 19

The muscle-bound goon returned. "Kane will see you now."

JD's face twisted, and he grumbled, having lost the bet.

The goon gave him a confused look. "Right this way."

He led us through the salon and up the steps to the foredeck where Kane lounged on a sun pad with stunning beauties on either side. There was a bottle of champagne nearby, and flutes with long stems dangled from manicured fingers. One of the girls fed Kane grapes.

He wore dark sunglasses, board shorts, and a gold chain dangling around his neck. Kane had short, dark hair, a square jaw, and chiseled features. He looked like he could have been a swimsuit model with washboard abs and toned arms. He was definitely living life like a king.

"I suppose you're here to talk about MC Sledge?"

"Whatever gave you that idea?" I said.

"It was no secret there was bad blood between us."

"Somebody filled him full of lead."

"It wasn't me or my crew. I can assure you of that. I'm a non-violent kind of guy."

I scoffed. "That's not the image you present to the world."

"There is perception, and there is reality. I'm just a happy-go-lucky guy who likes to enjoy life." He smiled. "Look around, deputy. What do I have to be upset about?"

One of the girls kissed him on the cheek. Not to be outdone, his other companion kissed him as well.

"You weren't upset about your collaboration going south?"

"Sure. I was upset and disappointed. But then I realized I shouldn't get upset because Sledge lacked the foresight to see my immense, untapped talent. I don't need to piggyback off his name to promote my music. I built a studio here, and I'm recording new tracks. I'll put them out on my own label. As you can see, I have the resources to market the material."

"Where were you the night of the murder?"

"I was right here. We had a party aboard the boat. There were 100 of my closest friends. I can give you a guest list. You can verify."

"He was here with us," one of the girls said.

"Yeah," the other girl said. "We had so much fun that night."

I looked at the muscle-bound guy. "What about you?"

"I go where Kane goes."

"Marcus is a loyal friend," Kane said. "He was here at the party all night."

"How convenient," I said. "You can all vouch for each other."

"In this day and age, nobody moves without leaving a trail behind them," Kane said. "Check the phone records. You'll see that none of us left the boat the entire evening."

"I'll do that."

"Marcus, compile a list of our guests and forward that to the deputy when you have time," Kane said.

Marcus nodded.

"Now, if you'll excuse me, gentlemen, I'd like to get back to enjoying my free time. Marcus will show you out."

"No need," I said. "I think we can find our way."

"Have a nice day, deputies," Kane said as we walked away.

Marcus followed us for good measure. We moved along an exterior passage on the port side to the aft deck.

"If you give me your number," Marcus said, "I'll text you a guest list for the party."

We exchanged numbers before leaving.

Marcus stayed on the aft deck as we crossed the passerelle and strolled down the dock.

"You buy his story?" JD mumbled.

"It's awfully convenient," I said.

I called Isabella.

"You getting anywhere with the Quinn Palmer case?" she asked.

"Not really," I said. "What about you?"

"Nothing. But I'm combing through her call logs, trying to get a picture of her movements over the last several weeks and see if I can make any correlations."

I told her about the DNA profile we discovered on the water bottle.

"Send me the data, and I'll see what I can find," Isabella said.

"While I've got you on the line, can you see if there were any cell phones present on Starfish Key the night of Sledge's murder?"

"I'll look for any devices that pinged the cell tower in that location. I'll get back with you."

"Thank you."

"And Tyson... Watch yourself. I've got a bad feeling about this."

"I'll keep my head on a swivel."

I ended the call, and we climbed into the Porsche. JD cranked up the engine and pulled out of the parking space.

"Where are you buying lunch?" I asked with a grin.

JD thought for a moment. "How about a little surf and turf?"

"Sounds good to me."

"How about *Five Fathoms*?"

It was an upscale eatery with a five-star chef and exquisite entrees that would easily put a dent in JD's wallet, covering the amount of the bet.

Denise buzzed my phone on the drive. "Phone company turned over the records from MC Sledge's account. A lot of calls to and from Lucas, a few with Darius Creel, and a few other random numbers. But there is one number that pops up frequently. Calls and texts at all hours."

"Who does it belong to?"

## 20

"Sonya Baldon," Denise said. "23. No criminal history. She's a dancer at *Forbidden Fruit*. Looks like the two had been communicating over the last several months."

"Sheldon had himself a girlfriend," I said.

"I think you're right. I don't have the content of their text messages, but I bet it's pretty juicy. I'll send you her current address."

"Thank you."

"And I'm sure you boys will have no qualms investigating Forbidden Fruit."

It was the premier strip club on the island.

"It's a tough job, but somebody's gotta do it," I said.

"Have fun," she said before hanging up.

I relayed the information to JD. A moment later, a text with Sonya's address buzzed through to my phone.

"How about we get the lunch buffet at Forbidden Fruit instead?" JD said.

The food wasn't nearly as good as *Five Fathoms*, but the scenery more than made up for it.

"We don't even know if Sonya's working today?" I said.

JD smiled. "Then we might have to make a few trips."

We drove to Oyster Avenue and parked at the curb. We hopped out and strolled the sidewalk, heading toward the adult establishment. Tourists wandered the avenue, and the smell of grilled food filled the air. There was never a dull moment on the strip, and the steady influx of tourists kept the bars and restaurants full.

We stepped inside the dim club, and the cashier waved us through. I'm not gonna say we were regulars, but we had been there enough for the cashier to recognize us.

Music pumped, and lights swirled the stage. The place smelled like whiskey and cheap perfume. Fog machines billowed smoke as a gorgeous beauty slinked around a chrome pole, her spike-heeled shoes accentuating her toned legs. She performed acrobatic feats, and all the patrons drooled.

We found the manager at the bar, and Jacko greeted us with a smile. He wore a shiny maroon sports jacket and black slacks. A gold chain dangled around his neck. He greeted us with a warm smile and a handshake—he always took care of us. "You boys here on business or pleasure?"

"A little of both," JD said. "We're looking for Sonya Baldon."

"She didn't kill anybody, did she?"

JD shrugged. "We intend to find out."

Jacko cringed. He pointed across the club. "The redhead. Her stage name is *Trixie*."

Sonya was in the middle of a lap dance, slinking her delightful body around an enthusiastic customer.

"Why don't you guys have a seat. First round's on the house. I'll have a waitress send Sonya over when she finishes up with her client."

"Much appreciated," JD said.

"What can you tell me about Sonya?" I asked.

He shrugged. "Nice girl. Keeps her nose clean. Hard worker. Comes in here, earns good money, and doesn't seem to get distracted. She's got a good head for business but terrible taste in men."

"Why do you say that?"

"Because her boyfriend is in here way too much. You know, the jealous, insecure type."

"Are they still dating?"

"I think so. I haven't seen him here in a few days. I don't really like it when the girls' boyfriends are around. The girls get a little inhibited. Customers don't have a good experience. Sometimes it leads to altercations. I had to kick her boyfriend out not too long ago."

"What did he do?"

"He got in a customer's face after the guy got a little too handsy with Sonya. He's done it a few times. We've got secu-

rity for that kind of thing. And if the girls don't mind, hey..."
Jacko shrugged.

"Did she offer any extra services?" I asked.

"I don't really know what she does in the Champagne
Room," he said innocently.

It was a diplomatic answer. Jacko wouldn't directly admit
that there was prostitution occurring in his establishment.
But, for the right price, things could be had in the Champagne Room. But that was between the girl and the client.

Vice would occasionally come in and make a sting. It was
mainly in response to complaints and to make it look like
they were doing their job. Somebody's wife would get
pissed, call their friend on the city council, outrage would
ensue, and pressure would come down on the department.
Things would tighten up for a while, then go back to normal
once the hubbub died down. *Forbidden Fruit* served a wide
range of clientele. Everything from college guys looking to
see the sights to celebrities and politicians—none of whom
wanted to see the best strip club on the island go out of
business.

We took a seat not far from the stage, and a cocktail waitress
in a skimpy little outfit with fishnet stockings approached
and took our order.

We watched the stage as men stuck dollar bills in G strings
and girls undulated in hypnotic ways.

The song ended, and the low, smooth voice of the DJ
rumbled the speakers. "Give it up for Houston!"

There was boisterous applause among the patrons.

"Please welcome to the stage, Crystal!"

A gorgeous blonde strutted the catwalk to the chrome pole, leaped into the air, and swung around like a circus performer—a very tight, toned, circus performer.

Sonya finished up with her client, put her bra and her skirt back on, took the cash, and stuffed it in her shoe. Our waitress whispered in her ear, and she looked in our direction.

I smiled and waved.

Sonya sauntered over and fell into my lap with a smile, draping her arm around me.

She felt good in my lap. There was no doubt about it.

"I hear you're looking for some company," she said.

"I'd like to talk to you about MC Sledge."

Her flirty smile faded, and her eyes brimmed. Flustered, she said, "I can't talk about him right now."

It was clear she had feelings for the man.

## 21

"I just can't do this right now." Sonya climbed out of my lap and wiped her eyes. She marched away, sobbing.

Another dancer came to her aid and tried to comfort Sonya. Her friend's accusatory eyes flicked to us, thinking we had upset Sonya in some way.

Jacko joined them and put a comforting hand on Sonya's shoulder. They spoke for a few minutes, then Sonya finally pulled herself together. She wiped her eyes, and at Jacko's urging, headed back toward us. She plopped into the chair across the table, her head low, her shoulders slumped.

Jacko gave me the thumbs up and a wink from across the room.

"I'm sorry," Sonya said. "I'm just really emotional right now."

"Understandable," I replied. "I take it you and Sledge were close?"

She nodded and sniffled, wiping her eyes again as they misted. "He was in the process of getting a divorce. He was gonna marry me."

"How did your boyfriend feel about that?" I asked.

Sonya's face tensed, and her eyes narrowed at me. "He's not my boyfriend."

"Are you sure about that?"

"I broke it off with Camden weeks ago."

"Before or after you started dating Sledge?"

Her face twisted. "Why does that matter?"

"I think Camden would think it mattered."

"I started dating Sledge a few months ago, but I didn't want to break up with Camden until I knew where it was going."

"Did Sledge know about Camden?"

She shook her head.

"I'm assuming Camden found out about your relationship?"

She hesitated. "Yeah."

"How did he take the news?"

"He was pissed. How do you think he took it?"

"Was he pissed enough to kill Sledge?"

She shook her head. "Camden wouldn't do that."

"How can you be so sure?" I asked.

She didn't say anything.

"Did Camden make any threats?"

She hesitated. "Yeah, but he always makes threats when he's pissed."

"Did he ever get abusive with you?"

She was silent.

"It's my understanding he was the jealous type."

"He could be, at times."

"And it never occurred to you that your infidelity might cause a problem?"

Her face twisted again. "I wasn't cheating on him. Not really. When I started sleeping with Sledge, I stopped sleeping with Camden. I never double-dipped."

"But you failed to tell Camden about your relationship. Meanwhile, I'm sure he got extremely curious as to why things dried up."

She cringed. "I'm just not really good with conflict, okay. I figured he'd get the message that I didn't want to be with him anymore."

"It might have been easier if you'd just told him."

"I did tell him. Last week. I said I needed my space."

"That doesn't sound definitive."

"It's not my fault if he doesn't want to believe I'd ever leave him."

"Do you know where Camden was the night of the murder?"

She shook her head again. "I think he was out with his friends that night."

"Where can we find him?"

"Well, we live together."

My eyes widened. "You broke up, but you still live together?"

"Well, I couldn't just kick him out. He's looking for another place."

"Where do you live?" I asked.

"The Delphine."

"Is he at your apartment now?"

She shrugged. "Maybe."

"Where does he work?"

"He doesn't have a job," she said with a sour face. "That's another reason I broke up with him. I'm tired of supporting his lifestyle."

"Is your name on the lease to the apartment?"

"It's my place, not his. I'm the only one on the lease."

"You mind if we search your apartment?"

She paused. "Sure. I guess so."

"Would you mind letting us into the apartment now?"

She shrugged and looked around. "I really need to work. It's turning out to be a good day. Plus, I don't really want to be there when you talk to Camden." She paused. "You can take my key and let yourself in if you promise to bring it back."

I exchanged a glance with JD.

"That will work," I said.

She dug the key from the lining of her bra and handed it to me. "Apartment #504. The passcode to get into the building is #2929." She frowned. "Are you going to arrest Camden?"

"If there's a reason to arrest him."

"You really think he could have killed Sledge?"

I shrugged. "You know him better than I do."

A grim look washed over her face.

I held up the key. "Thank you. I'll bring this back."

She nodded as concern bathed her face.

We left the table and spoke with Jacko before leaving. The bright sun outside was a stark contrast from the dim, seductive club. We'd forgotten all about lunch.

"Cute girl," JD said as we walked the sidewalk to the car. "But I sure as hell wouldn't want to date her. She needs to get her priorities straight. She sure has a strange definition of *not cheating.*"

"That sounds like motive enough for murder," I said.

We climbed into the Porsche and headed over to the Delphine. It was a luxury apartment complex, filled with trendy twenty-somethings. We pulled into the visitor's parking lot, hopped out, and punched in the access code at the call box. The lobby door buzzed, and JD pulled it open. We pushed inside and made our way to the elevator banks. JD pressed the call button, and a few moments later, we were on the fifth floor. I figured there was a good chance Camden was in the apartment.

We banged on apartment #504 and waited for a reply.

## 22

I banged on the door a few more times, but nobody answered. I used the key and unlocked the door, pushing it open cautiously. I shouted into the apartment, "Coconut County! Is anybody here?"

There was no response.

We pushed inside, and JD closed and locked the door behind us. We moved down the entrance foyer into the living room. The apartment had a standard floor plan with a small kitchen and a living room with sliding glass doors that opened to a balcony. There was a bedroom with a master bath. The place was decorated with modern furniture, and there were several framed sketches of ballerinas in graceful poses.

The pillow and blanket made it apparent that Camden had been crashing on the couch. The coffee table was littered with beer cans and empty plates with crumbs. He wasn't too good about looking after himself.

We moved into the bedroom and rummaged through the drawers and closet. I found a small bag of weed in a nightstand drawer. I didn't care about the weed. I was looking for a murder weapon.

Jack searched the closet but came up empty-handed.

Well, I shouldn't say *empty-handed.*

He found a box of sex toys, lube, handcuffs, and various other adult items. JD had a devilish smirk on his face. "Sonya might be fun to date after all."

"Put that back," I scolded.

He frowned, but put the items away.

I left Jack in the bedroom, moved back to the living room, and searched around the couch. I looked underneath the cushions and found an N9 submachine gun and a 9mm pistol.

The Novikov-9 was a Russian-made, blowback-operated, semi-automatic pistol that was a favorite among gangsters and mass shooters. They were capable of accepting large-capacity magazines. Compact and powerful, the weapon was banned in several states. The original manufacturer was long out of business, but there were plenty of units still on the secondhand market, and there were several unauthorized clones in circulation with their resurgence in popularity. You could find receiver designs online that could be 3D printed, and the units could be converted to fully automatic with relative ease.

With the number of bullets at the scene, I began to think the N9 was most likely the weapon that killed MC Sledge.

Ironically, the weapon's popularity exploded when it was featured in MC Sledge's video *Suck on my 9*. The video went viral with almost a billion views.

Honestly, they were junk. The accuracy sucked, and they were prone to jamming. But those minor details seemed to be of little concern to wannabe gangsters. It was all about looking cool.

I pulled on a pair of nitrile gloves and picked up the gun. I pressed the mag-release button and dropped the magazine. It was empty. I smelled fresh gunpowder when I sniffed the barrel.

I was pretty sure we had our guy. A sense of accomplishment and satisfaction filled me.

That's when I heard the lock jiggle.

The door swung open.

Camden stepped into the entrance foyer. His eyes widened when he saw us. He drew a pistol from his waistband and took aim down the corridor. "What the fuck are you doing in my home?"

## 23

"Coconut County!" I said, not making any sudden moves.

The barrel of Camden's pistol stared at me.

"Sonya gave us permission to be here," I said.

"I didn't give you permission to be here, mother fucker!"

"Put the gun down so nobody gets hurt."

JD lingered out of sight in the bedroom with his weapon drawn.

"Sonya is the leaseholder," I said calmly. "Let's not escalate the situation."

"How do I know you're a cop? You don't look like no cop."

"Put the weapon down, and I'll show you my badge." I was still holding the N9, though it wouldn't do much good empty. "I'm gonna set this down. Then I'm gonna reach for my badge. I would feel a lot better if you pointed that weapon somewhere else in the meantime."

Camden's face was tight, and he swallowed hard. He looked down the barrel, keeping me in his sights. He was 6'2", athletic build, short hair. I got the distinct feeling this wasn't the first time he had pulled a gun on someone.

I placed the N9 on the sofa, then slowly reached for my badge and pulled it from my pocket. I flashed the shiny gold thing in his direction.

"What if that's fake?" Camden shouted.

I rolled my eyes. "You're right. I broke into your house, planning to steal your guns, disguised as an undercover cop. You got me."

Camden's brow crinkled.

"Now put the gun down before you hurt yourself."

He stared at me for a long moment.

I could sense JD in the other room, ready to strike.

Camden finally knelt down and set the gun on the tile in the entrance foyer.

"Smart move," I said.

He stood tall.

"Kick the pistol into the kitchen," I commanded.

He frowned but complied. The gun slid across the tile.

"Alright, get down on the ground and put your hands behind your head."

"What for?"

"You're under arrest for the murder of MC Sledge."

His face twisted. "I didn't kill nobody."

JD emerged from the bedroom and swung the barrel of his pistol down the foyer toward Camden. "On the ground! Now!"

Camden's eyes flicked to JD, then back to me. He hesitated for a moment, then turned around and sprinted out of the apartment.

I launched to my feet and bolted after him.

He tore ass down the hallway and pushed into the staircase. His footsteps smacked against the concrete steps, echoing throughout the stairwell.

I raced to the end of the hall and plowed through the steel fire door, spiraling down the switchback staircase after him.

We plummeted down to the ground floor.

Camden hit the landing, then barreled through the door, stepping into the lobby.

I chased after him as he burst through the main doors and sprinted across the visitors' parking lot.

JD wasn't far behind.

My legs drove me forward, my chest heaving for breath.

Camden rounded the hedges and sprinted down the sidewalk. The guy was fast. He gave a quick glance over his shoulder, and his round eyes connected with mine.

Camden cut a hard left at the next corner and sprinted down the sidewalk. He weaved through tourists, bowling some of them over, racing past palm trees that lined the walkway. He darted into the street and clotheslined an oncoming guy on a moped. The guy flew off the back of the vehicle and smacked the concrete. The moped curved and plowed into a rack of bicycles on the other side of the street.

Camden scurried to the moped, but by the time he got it upright, I tackled him to the ground. We tussled for a moment as tourists gawked.

Somehow the squirrely little bastard slipped away. He sprang to his feet and took off running just as JD arrived, drawing down on him with his pistol.

As much as Jack would have liked to, he wasn't going to shoot an unarmed man in the back running away.

I launched to my feet and gave chase.

Camden sprinted down the block.

The area was congested. At the next stop sign, there were several restaurants and tourist attractions.

Camden pulled a fat security guard out of a golf cart at the stop sign. He hopped in, mashed the pedal, and the electric cart zipped around the corner.

We bolted around the corner, continuing our pursuit.

Camden veered into the opposite lane of traffic to avoid the line of cars that were backed up. The road was blocked off ahead due to construction, and there was nowhere for him to go. He veered left and sped down a narrow lane by the boardwalk that ran along a marina filled with sailboats and catamarans.

We raced past another apartment complex and more rows of bicycles chained to racks.

We couldn't keep up with the electric golf cart.

It zipped down the lane, made the turn at the next corner, and disappeared.

I thought he was gone for good.

A moment later, I heard tires screech and the crunch of plastic against metal.

## 24

B its of plastic and debris littered the street. A Super Duty truck had plowed into the little red golf cart. It had been spun around and was on its side. The wheels were twisted at unnatural angles, and Camden had been thrown from the vehicle. His body lay in the street motionless with his face against the hot concrete.

Blood oozed.

His arms and legs were splayed in odd directions. The crowd had gathered around, gawking with terrified faces and wide eyes. The driver of the truck hopped out of the vehicle and rushed to Camden. He dialed 911 as we arrived.

I knelt down and felt for a pulse. It thumped against my fingertips.

Camden was alive but unconscious. He clearly suffered head trauma from either the impact with the truck or the impact with the ground. His body was dotted with multiple cuts and abrasions, and I was quite sure he had a few broken bones. I didn't know what condition his spine was in and knew better than to reposition him.

I backed away and let the EMTs and paramedics take over when they arrived.

"Man, he came out of nowhere," the driver of the Super Duty said. "He ran the stop sign. I plowed right into him." Nervous sweat coated his skin. His eyes were wide, and he fidgeted, adrenaline coursing through his veins. "Think he's gonna be alright?"

Camden was far from alright. I wasn't sure he'd pull through.

"I don't know if I could live with myself if I killed somebody."

The driver was mid 40s with reddish-gray hair, a slender build, and a narrow face. He wore a white button-down, pressed wrangler jeans, and boots. He told me his name was Henry.

"It was an accident," I said, trying to reassure him. But if Camden died, or lived with disabilities, I'm sure it would haunt Henry for a long time.

"He didn't stop. He didn't even look!"

There were a few dents and scrapes on the Super Duty, but for the most part, it looked unscathed. There was a cracked headlight, and red paint streaked across the front bumper of the pearl truck.

Mendoza and Robinson arrived and managed the crowd. They took a statement from Henry.

Paris Delaney showed up with a news crew and grabbed footage of the gruesome scene. She spotted me and made a beeline for us. The camera lens soon hovered close to my face.

"I should have known I'd find you here," Paris said.

I tried not to show my displeasure with being on camera at the moment. I assumed it was rolling. It always was. Paris never wanted to miss a moment.

The gorgeous blonde slipped into her lofty reporter voice. "Deputy Wild, what can you tell us about the situation?"

The boom microphone hovered over my head, held by an assistant off-camera.

"We were in pursuit of a suspect when he stole a golf cart and recklessly endangered his life and the lives of others."

"Can you identify the suspect?"

"That's all I can say at this time."

"Is this suspect connected to the homicide of MC Sledge or the woman found at the Seven Seas?"

"I can't comment at this time."

"Do you think the situation could have been avoided?"

"Yes, easily."

"How so?"

"Don't run when you're under arrest."

"Would you agree that situations like this highlight the flaws in the department's pursuit policy, putting not only suspects but citizens at risk?"

My jaw tensed. "I have no comment on the department's policy. It's the duty of law enforcement to apprehend suspects that pose a danger to society."

I walked off camera.

Paris stepped into the frame and finished the segment. "We'll keep you updated as this story develops. Live, from Coconut Key's Historic Seaport, I'm Paris Delany."

She signaled the cameraman to cut. He lowered the camera from his shoulder and relaxed.

The EMTs finally stabilized Camden enough to move him. They loaded him into the ambulance and closed the rear doors. The siren chirped, and the red and white lights flickered as the ambulance pulled away from the scene, crimson blood still staining the road.

The crowd dissipated.

Henry climbed into his truck and drove away.

The news crew loaded their gear back into the van, and Paris trotted to me as we were about to leave.

I gave her a dirty look and started walking back toward the apartment complex.

"Tyson!" she called after me.

I ignored her.

Her high heels clacked against the concrete as she rushed alongside me.

"Can we talk? Off the record?"

I gave her a suspicious look. Nothing was ever off the record with Paris. "Why do you do that?"

"Do what?"

"Cause trouble."

"I'm not causing trouble. I'm just reporting the facts."

"You stir up drama at every opportunity."

She smirked. "That's my job, Tyson."

"Your job is to report the news."

She rolled her eyes. "My job is to entertain and to sell advertising."

"You can't really be serious about wanting us to stop chasing criminals that resist arrest."

Her face crinkled. "No, but it makes for good TV."

I shook my head and left her on the sidewalk. JD and I continued back toward the Delphine. Tourists walked the boardwalk and ate at cafés—most of them oblivious to what had just happened.

"Don't let her get under your skin," JD said. "That wasn't our fault."

"I know," I sighed. "But this kind of thing is completely avoidable."

"We're all responsible for our own decisions. Camden made a bad one when he decided to run. End of story."

I looked at my elbow, which was red and bloody from the nasty road rash I had acquired when I tackled Camden to the ground. The adrenaline had masked the pain, but now it was wearing off and starting to sting. My elbow and forearm were crusted with blood.

We made our way back up to the apartment and collected Camden's weapons as evidence. I washed the blood off my arm in the sink and blotted it with a paper towel before leaving. We headed back to the station, logged the evidence, and filled out after-action reports.

I wasn't looking forward to telling Sonya about the accident.

## 25

I braced for the worst.

We met Sonya at the hospital. The staff had contacted her upon Camden's arrival. She was listed as his emergency contact.

Sonya sat in the waiting room under the gloomy fluorescent lighting. The place was pretty crowded for an afternoon. There were people with broken bones, heavy coughs, abrasions, and crying children. Sonya had a blank look on her face. She had changed out of her skimpy little costume and into shorts and a tank top.

I was surprised that she didn't yell at us when she saw us. She simply asked, "What happened?"

I told her the details.

"Dipshit," she muttered in regard to Camden.

I handed her the apartment key.

"Did you find what you were looking for?"

"We found two weapons that may have been used in the murder. We'll know more when the lab runs ballistics."

Her brow lifted, and her eyes widened. "So, he killed Sledge?"

"We don't know that yet. Have you spoken with the doctor?"

"Camden's in emergency surgery now. That's all I know."

"You know where he got the weapons?"

She shook her head. "I knew he had a few guns, but I told him I didn't want to see them. They freak me out."

"He was carrying when he came back to the apartment. Is there any particular reason he'd need to carry a gun?"

She shrugged, but I could tell she was holding something back.

"What was he into?"

She hesitated for a moment, and her face crinkled. "He was dealing a little bit on the side. Nothing major. But I told him, do not bring that stuff around the apartment."

"You know who his supplier is?"

"No, and I don't want to know."

The surgeon pushed through the double doors and stopped at the front desk. He wore teal scrubs, a surgical cap, and his mask dangled around his neck.

The receptionist pointed out Sonya, and the surgeon ambled in our direction. "Sonya Baldon?"

She nodded.

"Camden suffered massive injuries and brain trauma. He has a broken arm, broken ribs, broken femur, and internal bleeding. He's stable, but he has a lot of swelling around the brain. He may require additional surgery to relieve the pressure."

"Is he going to make it?" Sonya asked.

The surgeon frowned. "It's hard to say. We're doing everything we can."

I flashed my badge and gave him my card. "Please contact me if he regains consciousness."

He took my card, nodded, and headed back to the patient area.

There was no need to put security on Camden. He wasn't leaving the hospital anytime soon.

Sonya's eyes filled. "He's going to die, isn't he?"

"I don't know."

"I gotta get out of here," she said, frazzled. "Hospitals give me the creeps."

She wiped her eyes and marched toward the exit. The situation was too much for her to process. The automatic doors slid open, and she was gone.

We left the ER and walked across the parking lot to the Porsche. An ambulance was parked at the curb. Not far away, a valet parking attendant handed a woman a ticket and hopped into her silver Lexus as she strolled in through the main hospital entrance. The sun hung high in the sky, cooking the concrete.

The unmistakable snap of a bullet filled my ear as it zipped past. It smashed into a nearby car window, webbing the glass with cracks and spraying shards in all directions.

I dove for cover between two vehicles, and JD did the same.

Two more bullets rifled through the air and smacked into the cars. Metal popped and pinged, and more glass showered down, sparkling in the Florida sun.

I crouched low and waited for additional fire. My hand grasped my pistol and drew it from my waistband. My heart pounded, adrenaline coursing through my veins.

I had a pretty good idea where the shot came from. I popped up over the car and angled my pistol, scanning the rooftop of the nearby parking garage.

There was nothing there.

My eyes dropped down, surveying each level below, finally scanning the ground-level.

I didn't see the shooter anywhere.

JD had taken cover behind the vehicle. He poked his head up with caution. "Parking garage."

"You see something?"

"No. But that's where I'd be."

We gave it another moment, then darted across the parking lot, crouching low between the cars, heading toward the parking garage.

We held up at the entrance to the first level, ducking below the concrete barrier that stood 3 feet high. I angled my pistol over the top, aiming my weapon toward the central staircase.

Tires squealed as a car spiraled down the ramp.

The driver gave a glance in my direction as he blew past and sped out the exit, turning onto the street. Horns honked. Tires of oncoming cars screeched, almost hitting the suspect's vehicle as he darted in front of them.

I ran to the street, but the white sedan was long gone. It turned at the next intersection and vanished into the city.

JD caught up with me. "You get a license plate?"

"Partial. XKR something."

I called Daniels. "Put a Bolo out on a white, four-door Honda sedan. Check the rental car companies and send the forensics team."

I filled him in on the details.

We pushed into the parking garage when I ended the call. JD took the elevator, and I took the stairs. With my weapon drawn, I spiraled up the staircase, just in case the guy in the car wasn't the shooter. I vaulted up to the top floor and swung the barrel of my pistol through the doorway, sweeping across the lot.

There were a few cars parked in the sunlight, but I didn't see anybody.

I left the stairwell and advanced toward the parapet that faced the uncovered ground parking where we had been fired upon. From this vantage point, the sniper would have had a clear shot.

At the base of the parapet was a single .300 Win. Mag shell casing. The shooter must have grabbed the other two but missed this one.

I left it where it was and waited for the forensics guys to document the scene.

A disconcerting feeling washed over me. It was clear that whoever killed Quinn was now trying to kill me. Either this was a message to back off the investigation, or this person was intent on killing Cobra Company operatives.

## 26

"You're not going to like this," Isabella said when I called.

I wasn't liking the situation as it was. More bad news was the last thing I needed.

"There's been a data breach. Sensitive information was compromised."

My jaw tensed, and I balled my hands into fists. I exhaled a frustrated breath. "Where was the data breach?"

"Not on our end."

"What's the extent of the compromise?"

"Unknown at this time."

"Do you know who's responsible?"

"Not yet. This could be a foreign government, or it could be hackers looking to sell the data on the open market. But from what I'm hearing, the breach is big. It's clear that a list of our operatives was compromised." She gave a solemn pause. "Michael Baker was found dead in his apartment half an hour ago in Chicago. He'd been there a few days by the time authorities found him."

I cringed.

This was hitting close to home. I knew Michael well.

"Make a list of all the ops the three of us ran together," I said. "One, in particular, comes to mind. Let's see if we can figure out who's got an interest in seeing us dead. I have a pretty good idea who, but let's see if we can get confirmation."

"I'll let you know what I find out. In the meantime, watch yourself."

"I will."

I ended the call.

"That didn't sound good," JD said.

"It's not."

"You recognize the guy driving the white car?"

I shook my head.

The forensics team snapped photos of the area and collected the shell casing. They also documented the scene on the ground-level parking lot and attempted to recover slugs from the vehicles. Deputy Mendoza interviewed the valet parking attendant.

We wrapped up and went back to the station to fill out more reports. Our lunch kept getting postponed, and by now, my stomach was in a knot, screaming for sustenance.

Daniels poked his head into the conference room as we typed away. "There's only one white Honda on the island with a license plate that starts with the letters *XKR*. Belongs to a guy named Jacob Richmond. The same guy that just called in a report of a gunman at the hospital."

My face crinkled with confusion.

"No priors. He's been living on the island for 10 years. Works at an old folks home. I seriously doubt that's your shooter."

"You got his number?"

Daniels gave it to me, and I called Jacob.

"This is Deputy Wild with Coconut County calling for Jacob Richmond."

"This is he."

"I wanted to talk to you about the report you just called in."

"Yeah. I was visiting my father in the hospital. When I was in the parking garage, I heard a couple of gunshots, so I hopped in my car and got the hell out of there. When I drove down the ramp to the first floor, I saw these two suspicious-looking characters with pistols. I thought they were gonna shoot me. I gunned it, peeled out of the parking lot, and almost got hit."

I rolled my eyes. "Did you see anybody else in the parking garage that looked suspicious?"

"No. Just the two losers on the ground level."

I stifled a groan. "And you didn't see anyone on the top level of the parking garage."

"I was never on the top floor. My car was parked on level 3."

"Thanks for your cooperation."

"Sure thing. Was anybody hurt?"

"No."

"I hope you catch those fuckers."

"We will get the responsible party," I assured before ending the call.

"Looks like you guys missed the shooter," Daniels said.

I frowned. "I wonder if the shooter stayed in the garage the whole time afterward. We didn't even bother looking." I shook my head, frustrated.

"You want to tell me what's going on?" Daniels said. "And don't give me that *classified* crap."

I hesitated for a long moment. I had a good idea who might be behind this, but I wasn't sure yet. "Sorry, I can't talk about covert operations."

The sheriff's face tightened.

"When I figure this out, I'll tell you the whole story," I promised.

He wasn't one to display emotion, but I could see the concern in his eyes. "Watch yourself out there. I've been to enough funerals this year already."

"Don't worry," JD said. "We're gonna find the son-of-a-bitch before he can cause more trouble."

It was an overly optimistic assessment of the situation.

"Maybe you two should lay low for a while," Daniels suggested. "Get out of town. Take that overgrown party boat of yours and go on a cruise."

JD's eyes perked up. "Now that's not a bad idea."

"This isn't a problem we can run from," I said. "Not for long. We'll draw out the assassin and take him down."

We finished at the station. Since JD was buying, he decided we'd go to happy hour at *Wetsuit* and grab something to eat and save *Five Fathoms* for another day.

I had eyes in the back of my head, constantly looking for threats—scanning rooftops, points of entry, alleys, etc. I kept a vigilant eye for suspicious-looking persons. It was all the things I did on a regular basis, taken to a new level of hyper-awareness. I plotted exit routes and defensive strategies for every situation I found myself in.

It's a good habit to get into.

I tended to look at life in contemporary society as divided into two time frames—*before craziness* and *after craziness*. Maintaining such a hypervigilant awareness for the average person was probably overkill in the BC era. But life wasn't normal anymore. Neither was society. The threat of mass shooters and domestic attacks made it a prudent course of action for the average person to be prepared for an extreme situation.

Just because somebody was trying to kill me didn't mean I was going to stop living my life. We've all got an expiration date, and that expiration date has a way of catching up with you no matter how hard you try to avoid it. You could spend your days hiding away in your home, protecting yourself from every possible threat, and an engine could drop from a plane and crash through your roof, squashing you like a bug.

Unlikely, but possible.

As they say, *life* is the leading cause of death.

We drove to Oyster Avenue, strolled into *Wetsuit,* and took a seat at a high-top table near the bar. I sat at an angle where I could watch the door. Though there was plenty of eye candy, I managed to maintain situational awareness. *For the most part.*

The waitresses wore bikini bottoms and tight-fitted neoprene tops, unzipped to their navels, exposing plump cleavage that could compromise the attention of even the most dedicated operatives.

We ordered sushi and a couple beers and tried to unwind.

After we ate, we left Oyster Avenue and headed to the warehouse district for band practice.

Denise called as we pulled into the parking lot. "I got news you're not gonna like," she said.

I groaned. How much worse could the day get?

## 27

"The guns you found in Sonya's apartment don't match the ballistics," Denise said. "Neither does the pistol Camden was carrying. He didn't kill MC Sledge. At least not with those guns."

A tight frown tugged my face. I shook my head with frustration. "Why the hell did he run?" I muttered to myself.

"Sorry to be the bearer of bad news," Denise said.

"Thanks for letting me know."

"Of course," she said in a cheery voice.

Denise could make bad news sound almost good.

I ended the call, and we strolled past the miscreants at the entrance and pushed into the warehouse. The band was tuning up as we stepped into the practice studio. I took a seat on the couch next to a pair of adorable groupies, put in my earplugs, and watched the show.

JD and crew ran through their setlist.

They had a show coming up at *Sonic Temple* over the weekend, and I was getting a little concerned that my newfound stalker's activities might spill over to my acquaintances.

I wasn't a hard guy to find.

Neither was JD. As the lead singer of an up-and-coming rock band growing in popularity, he was in a vulnerable position on stage. And we didn't have the resources to thoroughly vet the fans before each show. It would be easy to smuggle in a weapon. I was glad he wasn't the intended target.

I knew there was no way JD would ever cancel gigs. As far as he was concerned, dying on stage as the result of an assassin's bullet was probably the second-best way to go.

After practice, we went to *Jellyfish* for a change of pace. The place had a trippy, psychedelic vibe. Glowing jellyfish hung from the ceiling, illuminating the club with dim, soft light. Downtempo music pumped through speakers, and the place had a relaxing atmosphere. It was the kind of place where you could find a secluded couch, fall into the deep cushions, and lock lips with an eager accomplice. The place swarmed with pretty people looking to make a physical connection.

The drinks weren't cheap, and it kept the riff-raff out. The place was known for its signature cocktail, which was slippery smooth going down but could certainly sting in the morning.

I stayed mostly sober, keeping a watchful eye. I can't say the same for the band. The drinks flowed, and JD picked up the tab. It didn't take long for Crash and Faye to slink off to a dark corner.

Styxx's eyes followed them, and his face twisted with a scowl. He bitched at JD. "How come he gets to date the hot bass player?"

JD shrugged.

"It's your rules, dude." Styxx clearly wasn't in the loop that JD had broken his own rule.

"Well... rules are meant to be broken."

"Yeah, but don't you see a problem with this? What happens when this thing goes south, and we have more shows left that she needs to cover?"

"I guess we'll have to find another bass player," JD said. "What do you want me to do about it?"

"I think you should say something. You're the de facto bandleader."

"I don't think JD's in a position of authority on this one," I said.

JD's eyes narrowed at me.

"Right. You're the manager," Styxx said. "You need to lay down the law. You need to play bad cop."

"It's just two more shows. I think their relationship can survive another two weeks. Then his cast is off, and everything is back to normal."

"I guess. But I'm just saying... It puts everything we've worked for at risk. I mean, after what happened in New York, we should have been looking for another replacement."

"Two more weeks. Two shows. Wild Fury will survive. Plus, she's good at what she does."

"What she does is cause discord," Styxx said. His face tensed, and his eyes shifted around, seeing who was nearby. He whispered over the music, "Look, man, she was coming on to me last night. Keep that between us because I don't want to start drama."

JD and I lifted a curious brow.

"Did anything happen?" I asked.

Styxx's face crinkled. "No. Of course not. I would never do that to Crash. But it took a great deal of willpower, let me tell you. I just worry that some of the other members in the band might not be as disciplined," Styxx said, his eyes flicking to JD.

"Trust me, I'm not going there anymore," Jack said.

"Anymore?"

Guilt washed over JD's face.

"Oh, man!" Styxx said with disappointment. "You too?"

JD shrugged sheepishly. "It just happened. The girl is hard to say *no* to. I guess I lacked willpower."

Styxx glared at him. "This is exactly what I'm talking about. This is a recipe for disaster! For all we know, Dizzy could have joined the club too."

JD and I exchanged a curious glance.

Styxx's interrogating eyes blazed into me. "You haven't, have you?"

I shook my head. "But it's not for lack of opportunity."

Styxx groaned. "I have a hard time believing that you would turn her down."

"It was a complex situation, and I put the interest of the band and my friends first." I smiled.

His eyes lingered on me another moment, just to be sure I was telling the truth. Satisfied, he said, "I'm gonna go find Dizzy and see what I can pull out of him." He drifted away, weaving through the hordes of revelers, looking for our guitar player.

"I think he's feeling left out," JD said.

"You're probably right."

"Hey, Faye is a free spirit, and I totally accept that," JD said. "She can do what she wants, and as long as everybody's on the same page, no harm, no foul."

Neither one of us was going to begrudge anyone a little fun. Just as long as people's emotions didn't get played with. But emotions were tricky things and had a way of flourishing all on their own—even if you didn't want them to. The whole *friends with benefits* thing seems to only last so long before one of the involved parties develops a lopsided attachment.

As JD and I discussed the merits of free love, a sultry brunette in a skimpy black dress sauntered toward me. She drew the eye like honey drew flies. She was sticky sweet. Her blue eyes sparkled, and her hair shined. Her full lips were slick and glossy, and her spike-heeled shoes stabbed the tile with each step.

She pranced toward me, almost in slow motion—her hair flowing, the music pumping. It was like something out of a music video. Too good to be true. Her eyes locked onto mine, and her lustful gaze never wavered. She had her target in her sights.

I casually glanced around to see if there was anyone else nearby she could have been stalking.

Nope.

She was coming for me. And I was delighted.

Until she threw her drink in my face.

The whiskey stung my eyes and dripped across my lips. Tasted like good whiskey, too. What a waste.

## 28

"Claudia sends her regards," the brunette said before sauntering away.

It took a moment for the shock to wear off.

JD grabbed a handful of napkins from a nearby table and handed them to me. I wiped my face and blotted my shirt.

"Who the hell was that?" JD asked. "And who is Claudia?"

A bewildered look twisted on my face. "I have no idea."

I tried to soak up the whiskey from my shirt, but it was still damp. I smelled like a distillery.

"Did you screw Claudia over?" JD asked with accusatory eyes.

"I don't know anyone named Claudia!"

"You spent the evening looking out for assassins. You should have been looking out for brunettes." JD's eyes followed the luscious vixen as she sauntered back to the bar. "Though I think I might let her kill me."

"Is that assault and battery?" I asked facetiously.

JD shrugged. "Possibly."

"I think this warrants further investigation."

"Do you need backup?" he asked with a grin.

"No. I think I can handle this one myself."

I composed myself and marched across the club. The brunette leaned against the bar and ordered another drink. She had a nice lean, which accented her marvelous backside. The skimpy little dress had horizontal slits on the sides which ran the length, revealing her bare skin beneath. It offered a nice view and made it clear she wasn't wearing a bra or panties.

I flashed my badge, trying to get to the bottom of this mystery.

"Coconut County, ma'am. I'd like to ask you a few questions."

She looked a little startled by the badge. "Are you going to arrest me?"

"Do you always throw drinks on strangers?"

"When they are bastards," she said with a sassy eyebrow.

My face twisted with confusion. "Excuse me, do we know each other?"

"No, and I don't intend on getting to know you."

"Who is Claudia?"

She scoffed and rolled her eyes. "It figures you wouldn't remember."

My curiosity was piqued. "Maybe you can refresh my memory."

"I'm not sure I should give you the satisfaction."

"Maybe I should arrest you for assault and battery, take you down to the station, and interrogate you."

"You'd like that, wouldn't you?"

"The real crime is wasting good whiskey."

"You think you're clever, don't you?"

"Not clever enough to see you coming."

She smirked.

"Where is Claudia?"

The brunette looked around the club. "I don't see her. She must have left after the show."

"I take it you two are close?"

"No, actually. I never met her before tonight."

"Yet you felt compelled to defend her honor by tossing a drink in my face?"

She shrugged. "It sounded like fun."

"Was it?"

"Yes. It was oddly satisfying."

"You must have a lot of pent-up frustration."

Her eyes narrowed at me. "Perhaps. But $300 to get revenge on a cocky, arrogant dickhead was too good to pass up. It felt like standing up for women everywhere. Plus, you kinda look like my ex. So, there's that."

I lifted an intrigued brow. "Claudia paid you $300?"

"And bought the whiskey." The brunette smiled.

"What does Claudia look like?"

"Blonde, blue eyes, petite. Gorgeous figure. You screwed up!"

"What did I allegedly do?"

Her face tensed, and her eyes blazed. "Something unspeakable."

"You'll have to do better than that."

"Banging one of her bridesmaids at the rehearsal dinner. That's low!"

I chuckled and shook my head. "Not me. You've got the wrong guy."

The brunette scoffed. "Yeah, right."

"I've never been engaged to anyone named Claudia. And I certainly didn't bang one of her bridesmaids."

"She said you'd deny everything."

"And Claudia pointed me out specifically?"

"Yup."

"You're sure she didn't point to someone else, and you got confused?"

"Not a chance. I confirmed that she was talking about the cute guy with the dude who looks like he's from that '80s rock band—what was their name?"

People were mistaking JD for the famous '80s rocker less and less these days and recognizing him as *Thrash*—the lead singer for Wild Fury.

"So you think I'm cute?" I asked.

"Slow your roll, Cowboy. I don't need your kind of drama."

"I don't have drama. Claudia, whoever she is, has mistaken me for someone else."

"A likely story," she said, her velvety voice thick with sarcasm.

"I think you got duped."

She arched an eyebrow at me. "I got duped? Why would some random woman pay me $300 to throw a drink on some guy she doesn't even know?"

"Maybe she made up the story just to get you to do it?"

"I don't know about you, but I could think of better things to do with $300. I'm sure watching me throw a drink on you was fun, but it couldn't have been *that* fun." She took a sip of her drink, and her lipstick stained the glass.

"I think the least you could do would be to buy me a drink."

She laughed. "I'm not buying you a drink. You might throw it on me in retaliation."

"Do I look like the type to do that?"

She squinted, sizing me up. "You swear that you don't know Claudia?"

"I swear."

She continued to eye me with suspicion.

"I don't think you realize what kind of trouble you're in. I mean, assaulting an officer is a serious offense. You could do time."

She scoffed. "I didn't assault you."

"You *battered* me, actually. People often get assault and battery confused. They are two separate offenses. The whiskey stung my eyes. You intentionally caused me bodily harm."

She rolled her eyes. "You'd seriously handcuff me and throw me in jail?"

I shrugged. "I might have to handcuff you. You look like a handful."

She lifted a curious eyebrow. "I'm probably too much for you to handle."

"I've handled much worse."

She bit her bottom lip. "I bet you have."

She stared at me for a long moment, then flagged down the bartender. "A round for my friend. Put it on my tab."

"Whiskey. Rocks," I said with a smile.

"This won't be considered a bribe, will it?"

"Do I look like I'd accept a bribe?"

She looked me up and down. "The jury's out. Are you a good cop or a bad cop?"

I smirked. "What do you want me to be?"

## 29

I think she wanted me to be a bad cop. After a few drinks, she suggested we find somewhere more secluded to *talk*. We found a plush couch in a cozy corner. She sat dangerously close.

I liked danger.

"Now I feel bad," she said. "I've ruined your shirt."

"It will wash out."

She leaned close and sniffed. "And you smell like whiskey. I'm so embarrassed."

The sweet scent of her perfume hit my nostrils. She lingered, her big blue eyes staring into mine. Her lips begged for attention, hovering inches away. Her soft breath tickled my skin.

"How can I ever redeem myself?" she asked in a deviously innocent voice.

"I'm open to suggestions."

She scoffed. "Get those ideas out of your mind," she said, pulling away, taunting me. "I know your kind, and I'm not falling for it."

"What's *my kind?*"

Her eyes stared into mine. "Charming, handsome, heart-breaking."

I smirked.

Her eyes narrowed. "Are you sure you don't know Claudia?"

"Maybe she gave you a fake name. I've never been engaged, and I'm loyal as the day is long. I like to have my fun, but when I commit, I commit. I'd never do something like that."

She regarded me with a healthy dose of skepticism.

"So, what are you doing here all by yourself? Prowling for unsuspecting victims to douse?"

She blushed. "I'm never going to live that down, am I?"

I shook my head.

"I'm in town with a girlfriend. We came down to blow off steam for a few days. She met a guy last night, and they are out on a *date*. I'm not going to spend my vacation in a hotel room. I thought I'd go out and have a little fun."

"You should be careful out alone."

"I can take care of myself."

"Where are you staying?"

"Why? So you can stalk me?"

I chuckled. "I don't think you have to worry about me."

"Oh, I definitely have to worry about you."

"I'm harmless," I said with a devious grin.

She scoffed again, knowing better. "Are you a real cop? You're not like some mall security guard seducing unsuspecting women with your *position of power*, are you?"

I laughed. "I'm a real cop."

"Let me see your badge again."

I showed it to her, the soft lighting reflecting on the gold surface. "That's a real badge."

She surveyed it closely and seemed satisfied.

A waitress passed by our cozy couch. "You guys need another round?"

The brunette shook her head. "No, thank you."

The waitress slipped away.

"I should probably go home before I do something stupid," the vixen said.

"Too late for that," I said.

Her eyes narrowed at me. "I really do feel bad, if it's any consolation."

"I'm just messing with you. I've enjoyed your company."

She tried to hide a grin. "You should probably get back to your friends," she said, glancing around. "They're probably wondering what happened to you."

"I'm quite sure they haven't thought twice about me."

She paused for a moment, then extended her hand in a formal gesture. "Well, Mister Deputy, it's been a pleasure."

I shook her hand. It was soft and warm.

"Coconut Key is a dangerous place," I said. "How about a police escort back to your hotel?"

She gave me a sassy eyebrow. "Oh, no! I'm not falling for that routine."

I raised my hands innocently. "No routine. Just a little security."

She rolled her eyes. "I know how that ends."

"How does that end?"

She gave me a long look.

I could see what she was thinking. "You have a dirty mind," I teased.

She scoffed. "Me!?"

"Yes, you."

"I think you're projecting."

I chuckled and shrugged. "Maybe just optimistic."

She smirked, leaned in, and kissed my cheek. "Good night, Mister Deputy."

Her lips on my skin sent a thrill down my spine.

She stood up and straightened her skirt.

"How do I get hold of you? You know, in case we get reports of random whiskey attacks."

She laughed. "In that case, I shouldn't give you my number. Goodnight, Deputy."

"How long are you in town?"

"Not long enough to start something with you."

She spun around and sauntered away. She had a nice saunter. My eyes were glued to her hips as they swayed, fantasizing about what could have been.

## 30

I got up, went to the restroom, then planned on looking for JD and the gang. But the brunette vixen was waiting for me at the end of the corridor that led to the restrooms.

"Forget something?"

"Yes." She planted her wet lips on mine. They were soft, and her tongue was slick. She was a good kisser. When we broke for air, she shrugged and said, "You only live once."

I couldn't disagree and decided to make the most of the moment.

We made out for a few minutes, oblivious to our surroundings. We melted into one another, and her warm body against mine sparked all kinds of naughty thoughts.

When we surfaced again, she said, "How about that police escort?"

I was happy to accommodate.

I took her hand and pulled her through the club. We wandered around and found JD. I told him my *investigation* required a more intimate interrogation of the suspect.

He had found enticing prospects of his own and stayed at *Jellyfish* with the rest of the band.

"We should probably go to your place, in case my roommate comes back early," the vixen said.

We caught a rideshare back to the marina. I still didn't know her name. We'd get around to formal introductions later. There were more pressing matters at hand.

We were all over each other in the backseat. My hands traced the curves of her body, grabbing plump mounds. She moaned and quivered with anticipation.

The driver looked insanely jealous.

He dropped us off at the marina, and I helped the brunette out of the back seat. She straightened her skirt, then took my hand.

I escorted her down the dock, the moon glowing overhead. Boats swayed in their slips, and the gentle sound of waves lapping against hulls filled the air.

We crossed the passerelle to the aft deck of the *Avventura*.

"This is your boat?" she asked with impressed eyes.

"I split it with JD."

"You're definitely a bad cop."

I chuckled and slid open the door to the salon.

Buddy greeted us excitedly, barking and bouncing. He spun in circles and wagged his tail. I knelt down and petted him, and he barked incessantly at the brunette, jumping on her.

I didn't blame him. I was about to do the same thing.

"Settle down, boy," I said. I apologized to the sultry vixen. "Sorry, he's excitable."

She smirked.

I led him out of the salon and put him in JD's stateroom with a bowl of food and water. I needed a little privacy. The little Jack Russell would sit there and watch if I let him.

I returned to the salon, and the brunette handed me a drink. She made herself at home, pouring two glasses from the bar. She lifted her glass to toast. "To throwing drinks on strangers."

We clinked glasses and sipped the whiskey.

"This is a really nice boat."

"Thank you. Would you like a tour?"

"I'd love one," she said.

I gave her the quick version, then we ended up in my stateroom on the bridge deck. By that time, we had finished the whiskey, and I set my empty glass on the nightstand beside the bed.

With my hands free, I was ready to resume more urgent activities. "Where were we?"

"I believe we were right here," she said as she pressed her body against mine, planting a luscious kiss on my lips. Heat radiated from her core, and my hands continued the exploration of her delightful curves.

She had my full attention.

We fell onto the bed, and pretty soon, her skirt was over her hips. Then it was off entirely. As my prior recon had confirmed, she didn't wear a bra or panties. There was nothing else to peel off.

Her skin was smooth as silk, and our bodies collided with passion. Moans of ecstasy filled the stateroom, and she more than redeemed herself. If this was the result, she could throw a glass of whiskey in my face anytime.

We wore ourselves out and collapsed beside each other, breathless and slick with sweat. Pleasure chemicals swirled in my brain, and I buzzed with dopamine and oxytocin, still heady from the whiskey. It was hitting me a little harder than I anticipated.

"You're definitely a bad cop," she said with a naughty grin. "I might have to get in trouble more often."

She lay beside me, stroking my chest with her delicate fingers. Her touch was soothing, but I began to feel a little woozy. I didn't think I drank enough to have the spins.

I got up to take a leak, and on my way back, my situation worsened. The room swirled, and the corners of my vision grew dim. My legs gave out, and the world turned upside down. I crashed to the deck, out cold.

I t served me right for not getting to know her name. Not that it would have made much difference.

I don't know how long I was out. It could have been five minutes or an hour. A day, maybe two. It was still dark outside, but the boat was moving. The engines rumbled, and the deck pitched and rolled ever so slightly—the gyro stabilizer keeping things steady.

My head throbbed, and my stomach was still queasy. It took a moment to get my bearings. From what I could tell, I still had my kidneys and major organs—always a concern after getting roofied by a gorgeous woman you just met in a bar. At least according to Internet lore.

My wrists were cuffed around the crossbar on the desk. It ran between the back legs and gave stability to the desk so it wouldn't wobble from side to side. The metal bar was bolted to the brushed aluminum legs. I couldn't go anywhere without pulling the desk around, and I couldn't quite stand up as I was underneath the desk.

For a little girl, the brunette had a surprising amount of strength. She was able to drag me across the compartment and secure me with my own cuffs.

I struggled against the desk to no avail. Brute force wasn't going to get me out of this one.

With my hands hanging around the bar, I couldn't reach my pockets. She'd taken my wallet, phone, keys, and pistol.

We cruised through the inky blackness for about 20 minutes, then the engine stopped. A few moments later, the brunette sauntered into the stateroom. "You're awake," she said, surprised. "How are you feeling?"

"Crappy."

"It took forever for the drugs to take effect. I didn't mind so much. You're pretty fun in the sack."

"Thank you. How about you release me, and we go at it again?"

She grinned. "As much as I would like to, I have other plans. I'm gonna hand you off and collect a paycheck. And I've already lined up a buyer for this boat. This really turned into a win-win."

"Glad it worked out so well for you," I snarked.

"At first, I was just going to kill you. Then I thought, why not have a little fun? You're worth more alive anyway, and it wasn't much trouble to get you into a compromising situation. You really should be more selective about who you bring home."

"Tell me about it."

"Thank God you boys always let the little brain do the thinking. It makes my line of work so much easier."

"Who are you working for?"

"Somebody who wants to see you and your friends dead and will pay extra to do it themselves."

"You killed Quinn, William Oliver, and Michael Baker."

"You catch on quick."

"You climbed the balcony to get into Quinn's hotel room."

"Like I said, you're smart."

"But the maid said a man asked to get into that room."

"I found a guy in the bar. Said I had a thing about sneaking into hotel rooms. I told him I'd blow him if he got us into the room next to Quinn's."

"That was his DNA on the water bottle."

"Like I said, you catch on quick."

"Why bother making Quinn's death look like a suicide?"

She shrugged. "I get bored easily. I need to keep it interesting. Plus, it's always kind of fun watching law enforcement chase their own tail." She sighed. "It's really a shame that you have to die. You were kind of fun."

"You don't have to hand me over."

She frowned. "I do. See, I've got this thing about loyalty. I don't break a contract ever. I'm sure you can relate." She looked at her watch.

"How much are they paying you?"

"Six figures. But don't even try to offer me more. I won't take it. Besides, I'm gonna make more off this boat than I am off of the contract for you, which has really got me questioning my line of work. I mean, this was easy. I could totally make a career out of seducing rich yacht owners and stealing their overpriced toys. It's way easier than targeting Cobra Company operatives." Her face crinkled. "But I've got to say, for as tough as you guys are supposed to be, this has been a cakewalk. I had a much tougher time hunting down some of the Red Hornet guys."

"You seem to know a lot about me, and I don't know anything about you. I don't even know your name."

"Like I said, you really should be more careful who you bring home. Some of these girls are crazy."

"I'm beginning to realize that. So, what do I call you?"

"You can call me bitch if you'd like."

I laughed. "Since I'm about to die, what's the harm?"

She surveyed me for a moment. "Call me Penelope."

Definitely not her real name.

*Penelope* looked at her watch again.

"Sector Underground," I said. "That's who hired you."

"I really don't know. I don't ask questions. The request comes in on an encrypted app. Funds are sent to my crypto wallet. I do the job. All communication is anonymous. I don't know the identity of the people hiring me. And honestly, I don't really care."

"You take whatever job comes your way? Doesn't matter whose side they're on?"

She scoffed. "Sides? You still think there are sides? You should know better than that. There is me, and there is everybody else. That's how the game is played."

"No friends, no close attachments?"

"Friends and close attachments get you killed. You should know that. If you don't trust anybody, you can never be betrayed."

"That's a lonely way to live."

"You're one to talk. Besides, do I look lonely? I can find company every night of the week."

"That's not what I'm talking about."

"Please, spare me. There is no such thing as a meaningful relationship. Everyone will leave you or betray you in the end. Life is a single-player game. We all die alone."

"That's a pretty cold worldview."

"It's a realistic worldview. Hence the reason why I'm still alive, and you're one step closer to your grave."

"Ouch," I said.

She looked at her watch again. "Now, if you'll excuse me, our friends should be arriving shortly. Don't go anywhere," she snarked.

I'd met some pretty cold, calculated killers in my day. *Penelope* ranked high among them. Was she a true sociopath, or was she just capable of compartmentalizing really well?

I reached my hands up and felt around the top of the desk.

The crossbar limited my reach, hitting my collarbone as I stretched up. I managed to topple a jar of pens that sat atop the desk. A few spilled onto the deck, but I couldn't reach them.

I felt around the desk and finally clasped a ballpoint pen. I brought it down, bent the metal clip at an angle then stuck it into the key slot on the handcuffs. I fumbled it around until I was able to trip the mechanism. The cuffs swung free.

I slid out from under the desk, released the other cuff, then darted across the compartment to my nightstand. I pulled open the drawer and grabbed another pistol. I pressed-checked the weapon, then advanced forward.

The barrel of my pistol led the way as I moved down the passageway, past the lounge and the theater room, creeping toward the helm. I grabbed the handle to the hatch and twisted slowly, just barely cracking it open. I peered through the windows of the wheelhouse and saw Penelope on the foredeck.

I slipped into the wheelhouse and pulled the hatch shut behind me. I crouched low behind the helm controls. Penelope had left my wallet, keys, and phone on the console. I quickly grabbed them.

Penelope was on the starboard bow, scanning the night for signs of her connection.

I crept to port, quietly slipped out the water-tight hatch, and edged forward along the port side passageway.

The moonlight glowed, and a nice breeze blew across the bow. The boat rocked gently.

I angled my weapon over the sun pads and took aim at Penelope's back. She had my pistol in her hand.

I was still a little unsteady from the drugs she'd given me, and the mild rocking wasn't doing wonders for my balance.

"The game's over!" I shouted. "Drop the weapon and put your hands behind your head. Turn around slowly."

She groaned but complied. The weapon clattered to the deck.

"Should have killed me when you had the chance. But you got greedy."

"You can't blame a girl for trying." She sighed. "What happens now?"

"I arrest you."

She frowned. "Sorry. That's not in the plan."

"No plan ever survives the battlefield."

I inched around the forward lounge, keeping my weapon aimed at the stunning vixen.

"You won't shoot me," she said.

"Want to bet?"

As I rounded the sun lounge, she took off running and plunged down the steps to the main deck.

She was partially right.

I wasn't keen on shooting an unarmed woman in the back as she fled.

I raced along the gunwale and snatched my pistol from the deck, then plunged down the steps to the main deck.

Penelope had darted inside through the receiving entrance. From there, she could have gone anywhere.

There were more goons on the way. I needed to neutralize the threat quickly.

I inched cautiously inside and swept the barrel of my pistol in all directions, clearing the immediate area. I sidestepped to the salon and peered in, quickly scanning the compartment.

I stood still, listening.

Buddy's muffled barks filtered from JD's VIP stateroom. I knew Penelope wasn't hiding in there.

I stepped to the crosswalk and inched toward the centerline, moving past the main staircase. A black high heel rested on the steps below. I figured she tossed them, perhaps as a decoy. Certainly to move silently.

I took a deep breath, trying to catch a subtle hint of her perfume.

I didn't smell anything.

I crept toward the galley and whipped the barrel of my pistol around the corner. I swept the compartment, then pushed inside and looked to see if Penelope was crouching behind the counter.

The galley was empty.

A crew staircase led below deck to the crew compartments.

There were endless routes she could have taken.

I backed out of the galley and stepped outside to the port passageway. My eyes scanned in both directions.

The passage was clear.

She was either above or below. I wondered if she had doubled back to the bridge deck. I moved forward, climbed the stairs, and emerged on the foredeck, back where this had started.

The barrel of my pistol swept the area.

That's when I heard the garage door open. I spun around and plummeted down the steps, moving aft. By the time I got to the stern of the boat, Penelope had launched the tender, jetting out of the port side tender garage. The engines howled, spitting a frothy white wake as the craft plowed through the swells. She looked back at me as I leaned over the gunwale, taking aim with my pistol.

I should have emptied the entire magazine, but I didn't.

She grinned and waved as she disappeared into the night.

## 33

I knew this wasn't over.

I ran inside and grabbed a set of night vision optics with IR from a storage compartment, then raced back to the port-side gunwale. I scanned the horizon with white-hot infrared and caught a glimpse of Penelope escaping in my tender. Coming in fast on her starboard side was a racing boat, skimming across the surface.

I assumed that was her terrorist connection.

There was no doubt Penelope contacted them with an update on the current situation. Even though her plan had been derailed, it seemed like the goons were closing in anyway. Sometimes, when a target is right there in front of you, it's too hard to resist.

The engines rumbled, and the racing boat sped in my direction, kicking up a rooster tail of frothy white water.

I dashed back inside and climbed up to my stateroom. I donned a bulletproof vest, grabbed a few flash-bang grenades, and my short-barreled AR-15 with a suppressor. It was decked out with a modular rail system that held an IR illuminator and tactical flashlight. I yanked the charging handle, chambering a round, and a satisfying clack filled the compartment. It sounded like imminent justice.

I darted out of the stateroom and plunged down the steps to the main deck. I stepped to the port side passageway and crouched low beneath the gunwale.

The speed boat raced toward the *Avventura* and circled the yacht.

There were three men wearing ski masks aboard. It was a 54-foot beast with five outboard engines. The thing was rocket-ship fast and could outrun just about anything on the water—the perfect vehicle for a quick strike.

I stepped back inside and moved aft toward the salon. I hovered in the passage, just forward of the salon, and dialed the Sheriff's Department. I updated the dispatcher with my situation. I launched the maps app on my phone and was able to get a general idea of where I was, but I didn't have my exact coordinates. There was no time to get to the helm station and look at the charts.

I left the phone connected, slipped it into my pocket, and readied my rifle. From where I stood, I had a clear view of the aft deck.

The racing boat pulled to the stern, and two thugs leaped onto the swim platform with assault rifles. The getaway driver stayed behind. The two goons climbed the steps to the aft deck and spread out, each taking an outside passageway.

The lights were out in the salon, and the tinted windows made it difficult to see in, which gave me a slight advantage.

The goons raced forward on either side of the boat.

I stepped into the salon as they passed and flattened myself against the forward bulkhead. I crouched low and angled my AR around the corner, down the forward port-side passageway, using a left-handed grip.

As the goons reached amidships, I heard the handle twist and the port-side hatch open.

I waited for the dipshit to step inside. He crept toward centerline, and when his silhouette appeared in front of my sights, I squeezed the trigger twice. Muzzle flash flickered, lighting up the passageway.

The goon twitched and danced as two bullets punctured his thoracic cavity. He fell to the deck with a groan and a gurgle as his lungs filled with fluid. His weapon clattered away.

I immediately swung my weapon in the opposite direction and moved to the starboard side, holding up just before the passageway. I took a breath and angled the barrel of my rifle down the starboard passageway and was met with muzzle flash.

I ducked behind the bulkhead for cover as bullets snapped down the corridor and rocketed across the salon.

I cringed at the sound of glass breaking.

## 34

I grabbed a flash-bang grenade from my tactical vest and lobbed it down the corridor. It bounced off the bulkhead at just the right angle to roll into the cross-corridor where the goon was.

I plugged my ears and sprinted to the port side.

The deafening bang rattled the bulkheads, and the blinding flash illuminated passageways like a strike of lightning. Smoke filled the compartment.

With my weapon in the firing position, I rushed forward down the port side passage, flanking the goon. I angled my weapon around the corner of the crosswalk at the disoriented terrorist. I fired two shots as he swung his barrel in my direction. Bullets peppered his chest, spraying volcanoes of crimson blood. He crashed to the deck, and the weapon fell away.

I moved across centerline, past the stairwell, to the starboard side.

The goon sucked heavy breaths, rattling as his lungs filled with blood. A moment later, he was gone. His chest had stopped heaving, and the awful sound of labored breaths ceased.

I knelt down and felt for a pulse just to be sure, then sprinted aft. I strode across the salon and pushed onto the aft deck.

The goon in the racing boat saw me and throttled up.

I took aim and squeezed the trigger, unloading the rest of my magazine. My weapon hammered against my shoulder, and smoke wafted with the breeze. Muzzle flash illuminated the area.

At least a few of my bullets hit their target because the driver slumped against the wheel. The racing boat plowed into the swells, full throttle. The rumble of the engines echoed across the water as it disappeared into the blackness.

I waited on the aft deck for the authorities to arrive. Before long, the area swarmed with Coast Guard patrol boats. *Tango One* pattered overhead. Daniels arrived with JD, Brenda, and the forensics team.

Daniels just shook his head when he stepped to the aft deck. "Maybe you should stop picking up random strangers in bars."

"So I've been told," I said.

"Can't you ever bring home a normal girl?"

I shrugged innocently. "She looked normal to me."

He gave me a doubtful glance.

"She looked like trouble," JD said.

I rolled my eyes. "She looked like a good time, and you know it."

"Often one and the same," JD replied. "Tell me you at least did the deed?"

"Oh, we certainly did that."

Jack grinned. "Is there going to be a second date?"

"I'd like to see her again," I said dryly. "On the business end of my pistol."

"By the way... the shell casing recovered from the parking garage didn't have any prints," Daniels said. "Your girl is smart enough to wear gloves when she loads."

"She's not my girl," I clarified.

Daniels tried to steer things back on track. "Tell me about the dead terrorists."

"She was going to hand me over to them. Apparently, I'm worth more alive than dead."

"That's debatable," Daniels said.

The forensics team snapped photos and collected shell casings and slugs. Brenda examined the bodies.

"I think it's time you tell me what's really going on," Daniels said. "No more bullshit."

I sighed and pulled him and JD aside. I spoke in a hushed tone. "There's been a data breach of classified information. It seems that whoever hacked the system is selling the information to the highest bidder. Two of my former colleagues are dead. I can think of a handful of operations the three of us worked together. One, in particular, went south."

JD and Sheriff Daniels listened intently.

"And you think someone is taking revenge?" Daniels asked.

I nodded. "What I'm about to tell you remains between us. This was many years ago. It was a hostage situation. Without going into too much detail, we were tasked with recovering a high-value asset that had been kidnapped. It was a pretty standard snatch and grab, but things got a little fouled up as they often do. Our asset had sensitive information, and we needed to extract him before the terrorists had an opportunity to break him. We recovered the asset, but the death toll was higher than expected. During the raid, several terrorists were killed. One of them happened to be the brother of Elias Fink. The head of Sector Underground."

JD's and the sheriff's eyes widened.

"I can't imagine that's somebody you'd want pissed off at you," Daniels said.

"With the data breach, he could have figured out the operatives involved in the raid that killed his brother," I said.

"The FBI and the CIA have been trying to track him down for years," JD said. "He blew up a federal building. Not to mention his involvement in the bombing of the *USS Intrepid*. There's a helluva bounty on him. I'd personally like to put a bullet in his head. I lost two buddies on the *Intrepid*."

"Don't forget about the two embassy bombings," I said.

Fink was a radical with extremist views which often seemed contradictory. He was an anarchist more than anything else.

After fleeing the country, he assisted several terrorist groups while maintaining Sector Underground which was operating around the globe. His loyal followers caused chaos and mayhem on command. Fink had amassed a great deal of wealth and used it to fund his terror campaigns.

"Hell, this might be an opportunity," JD said. "Follow the money. He hired the hitter, so there has to be some kind of trail."

"It's all just speculation at this point," I said. "I don't have confirmation."

"And you think these two dead guys are part of Fink's organization?" Daniels asked.

"We'll find out soon enough," I said.

JD and Daniels followed me inside the salon. We made our way down the starboard corridor to the fallen goon. Brenda had removed his ski mask.

With my phone, I snapped a headshot. I took a photo of his companion as well and sent the images to Isabella. I texted: [These guys just tried to kill me.]

## 35

I told the forensics guys to dust the place for prints, including all the whiskey glasses. I was pretty sure I knew *Penelope* was smart enough to clean up after herself. Then again, maybe not.

It didn't take Isabella long to call back.

"Tell me you got something," I said.

"Got a match on facial recognition. Both have ties to Sector Underground, but they're not pros. Previous arrests for destruction of property, resisting arrest, general mayhem."

"That's why Fink hired the hitter. These were just collection guys. The real assassin is still out there."

"It seems you're an important target," Isabella said.

"She probably gave me a fake name, but see if you can find any intel on a hired gun named Penelope."

"She sounds interesting."

"She is."

"Want to tell me about her?"

I filled her in on the details.

"Okay, that puts her at the top of my most-wanted list, along with Fink," Isabella said. "What else can you tell me about her?"

I gave Isabella a description of the brunette vixen. I told her the forensics team was dusting for prints now.

"She shouldn't be too hard to find," Isabella said.

"If anybody can track her down, you can."

"And when I do, I want her dead. Can you handle that? Or have you developed a soft spot?"

"You know I'm trying to avoid killing people unless they absolutely, positively deserve it."

"I think she qualifies."

I couldn't disagree.

"I'll be in touch."

I ended the call and slipped my phone back into my pocket.

Once the forensics guys had documented the scene and the bodies were removed, we all headed back to Coconut Key. The Coast Guard found the terrorists' speedboat a few miles away. It had apparently hit a wave, gotten airborne, and flipped over. The body of the getaway driver still had not been discovered. I figured he was shark bait.

JD manned the helm as I swabbed the deck, cleaning up the blood. Of course, Fluffy had stepped in a puddle of blood and tracked it all over. The ends of the white cat's fur were stained with crimson, and I was sure she'd give me a fit when it came time for a bath.

A bullet was lodged into a pane of the sliding glass door. The flash-bang grenade had marred the surface of the deck and blemished the nearby bulkheads. Other than that, the boat hadn't suffered too much damage.

With the mess cleaned up and the threats diminished, I let Buddy out of Jack's stateroom. He barked, bounced, and licked my face.

I knelt down and loved on him. "I know, boy. I should have listened. She was trouble," I said, baby talking him. "She's not coming back over. I promise."

Buddy barked twice.

The little guy always made me smile.

By the time we got back to the marina and connected shore power and water, the sun was cresting the horizon, and I was ready for a little shut-eye.

I decided to fix breakfast first. I put on a pot of coffee for JD and whipped up omelettes, hash browns, and bacon.

"Think Penelope's gonna make another attempt to take you out?" JD asked.

"If she's as dedicated as she says she is, I would assume so. Though I don't think her employer is too happy with her right now."

"If she doesn't finish the job, someone else will," JD said with a grim look on his face.

It was a fact that I was well aware of.

"We might just have to cut this off at the source," he said casually as he sipped his coffee.

I was beginning to think he was right.

"I'm just saying, two can play at this game. You know I'm down for whatever."

"I know," I said.

I was lucky to have a friend like JD. No matter what, he would be right there, leading the charge. There was no scheme too crazy, no odds too remote. He was all in. And he knew he could count on me for the same. But I wasn't exactly ready to go halfway around the globe to track down some angry leader of a terrorist organization. There was no telling where Elias Fink was hiding out.

"I'll stick around and take watch while you sleep," JD said.

I needed eyes in the back of my head at the moment, so I wasn't going to turn the offer down.

I crawled off to my stateroom after breakfast and caught a couple hours of sleep. It was that thin, anxious sleep, always on the verge of waking—the leftover remnants of adrenaline still coursing through my veins. Plus, the remnants of the drug left me feeling less than optimal.

Denise called around noon. The phone buzzed on the nightstand, and I snatched it, swiped the screen, and put the phone to my ear, my eyes still glued shut.

"I heard you had an interesting evening," Denise said in a sassy tone.

"Jealous?"

"Dream on," she said.

She wasn't going to admit it, but there was a hint of jealousy in her voice.

"Are you calling to reprimand me for my poor judgment?"

"No, I'm calling to tell you that your little plaything left a fingerprint on a whiskey glass.

That opened my eyes. "Did you get any hits in the database?"

"No. But something really strange just happened. After I ran the print, I got a call from Agent Conroy with the CIA."

"Not entirely surprising."

"He wanted to know where I acquired the prints."

"Did you tell him?"

"I told him in the course of a routine investigation. He pressed for details. I said I'd have my superior call him back. Your friend is definitely on someone's radar."

I laughed. "Now more than ever."

"I'm gonna send you the print. Send it to your contact. My curiosity is piqued. Let me know what you find out."

"I will. Thank you."

The fingerprint data came through a moment after I hung up. I texted the file to Isabella.

She called back a few minutes later.

## 36

"Looks like your lady-friend's real name is Sophia Breslin," Isabella said. "Quite an impressive resume. Had a support role with Special Forces, then worked at the DIA. Bounced around the intelligence community for a while until she was blacklisted. Now she contracts with an organization called *Phantom*."

"Phantom?"

"Crowdsourcing for assassins and clandestine operatives. It's the brainchild of Helmut Wolff. The app is encrypted and decentralized. It can't be shut down. It connects clients with operatives all over the globe. Payments are made in crypto, and Phantom takes a percentage. It makes killing as easy as ordering a pizza. It's the future of terrorism."

I groaned.

"Something tells me we're going to see a lot more Phantom operatives."

"Great."

"I'll be in touch. Stay safe."

I ended the call and pulled myself out of bed. I took a shower, got dressed, and found JD. He hung out on the sundeck, catching rays, drinking a beer.

He grinned. "I've been keeping a vigilant watch, and so far, I have detected no threats."

"You look like you've been working hard."

"I have. I took Buddy out for a walk. Your pets are all fed and watered. And I've worked up an appetite. Let's go grab something to eat. I'm starving. And I need a change of scenery."

"Where do you want to eat?"

"I'm thinking Juicy Burger."

"Okay."

JD climbed out of the lounge chair, gulped down the last swig of beer, and tossed the bottle in the trash. We headed down to the main deck.

"Isabella ID'd our spy friend," I said.

"*Your* spy friend," JD corrected.

I updated JD and gave him the details.

"Maybe you can put a contract out on her?" JD suggested with a grin.

"Tempting, but I'll handle this one myself."

"It's the gig economy for killers," JD mused. Then his face soured. "Though I'm sure you get what you pay for. It's like when you hire a rideshare to the airport. The driver just sits in his car. He doesn't get out and get your bags. He doesn't help you to the curb at the airport. It's the little touches that are missing. Customer service is important."

"Murder with a smile," I joked.

We walked down the dock, and JD clicked the alarm to the Porsche. The lights flashed.

I paused before getting in.

JD read the trepidation on my face. "Don't worry. She's been in my line of sight all morning. Nobody placed any car bombs. Besides, they're after you, not me."

He smiled and pulled open the car door.

I hopped into the passenger seat, and I was relieved once JD cranked up the ignition and the car didn't explode.

"She's probably long gone," JD said. "Hell, she bugged out at the first sign of trouble."

"Runaway to fight another day."

We drove to *Juicy Burger* and chowed down on greasy cheeseburgers and sweet potato fries. It hit the spot.

The day had evaporated. I felt terribly unproductive, but then a day of lounging around was probably called for after recent events. A lazy afternoon with no drama was just what the doctor ordered.

"Why don't we take the afternoon and go fishing?" JD suggested. "Do a little treasure hunting while we're at it."

He wouldn't get any complaints out of me on that front.

Jack paid the tab, and we left the restaurant. As we walked across the lot toward the Porsche, a man and a woman in a pearl Lexus pulled from a nearby parking space and drove past us. In my current state, I was hyper-aware of everything. The couple didn't look like assassins, and my momentary spike of adrenaline faded.

They exited the parking lot and stopped at the light on the corner. That's when two thugs with angry weapons accosted them.

"Out of the car now, mother fucker!" a goon shouted as he aimed his gun at the driver.

Everything happened in the blink of an eye.

I drew my pistol and raced toward the street.

The man driving the pearl vehicle hesitated, then unlocked the door and opened it. To the thug's surprise, the driver had a pistol in his hand and was about to pop off a few rounds.

## 37

The goon responded quicker.

Muzzle flash flickered from the barrel, and a short burst of fire erupted from a submachine gun. The bullets peppered the driver, and crimson blood splattered the windshield.

The woman in the passenger seat screamed.

The thug pulled her husband out of the car, and his body flopped to the street. The goon hopped behind the wheel and pulled the door shut.

The woman screeched in hysterics, her shrill voice filtering out of the vehicle.

The goon aimed his weapon at her. "Dumb bitch, get out of the car!"

His accomplice pulled open her door and yanked her to the street.

"Freeze!" I shouted, racing toward the scene with my weapon drawn. "Coconut County!"

The driver of the vehicle dropped the car into gear and floored it before his accomplice could hop in. Tires spun, and smoke wafted from the wheel wells. The smell of burned rubber drifted on the breeze as he barreled around the corner, leaving his accomplice chasing after the vehicle, the passenger door still open.

The engine howled, and the pearl car screamed down the street, squealing around the next corner.

The accomplice took off running, and I gave chase.

He dashed across the intersection as traffic began moving again.

I got stuck at the light until there was a break in the flow. I launched across the crosswalk to the median and held up again as more traffic whizzed by.

The perp kept running.

Horns honked as I sprinted in between vehicles, crossing the road, following the thug down the sidewalk.

He looked over his shoulder with wide eyes, then took a hard right at the next intersection.

I made the turn a moment later and continued after the perp.

He dashed across the street when the traffic broke, and I followed. He turned at the next block, disappearing behind a building.

My legs drove me forward, running as fast as I could. I turned at the intersection and followed the scumbag.

He crossed the street and darted into an alleyway. I heard his footsteps echo off the narrow walls.

When I rounded the corner into the alley, a spray of bullets erupted. I dove for cover, bullets snapping past my ears.

The perp took off, exited the alley, and turned down the next street.

I pushed off the concrete and sprinted down the passage. *The little bastard just got on my bad side.*

I held up at the mouth of the alley and peered around the corner, not wanting to get caught by another spray of bullets from his submachine gun.

The thug raced down the sidewalk, and I continued pursuit.

He angled the weapon over his shoulder and squeezed the trigger again.

I ducked behind a parked car as more bullets streaked through the air.

After a moment, I launched from behind the parked car and continued down the sidewalk.

The perp looked over his shoulder once again and swung his weapon in my direction.

Wham!

A silver sedan plowed into him as he stepped into the crosswalk without looking.

The grill smacked into his legs, tumbling him onto the hood with a thunk. His body made a deep impression in the thin metal. The impact spun him around, smacking him into the windshield and launching him a few feet into the air. His body crashed back down atop the roof.

Metal popped and pinged.

His body lay motionless on the roof like a limp noodle.

The driver panicked—her eyes wide, her hands covering her mouth. She hesitated for a moment, then punched it.

I guess she didn't want to deal with the drama. She probably didn't realize this guy was a fleeing suspect. Tires squealed as the sedan rounded the corner and sped away.

The perp rolled off the roof, smacked the trunk, then flopped to the concrete.

I tried to make a note of her license plate as I ran toward the perp. I knelt down beside his motionless body and felt for a pulse in his neck.

Judging by the unnatural angle of his legs, he had a broken femur. He, no doubt, suffered multiple broken ribs and a concussion. Bruising was already setting in. The compound fracture of his left arm was particularly gruesome. The white bone protruded from his skin, drenched in blood.

I dialed 911 and waited for the ambulance to arrive.

## 38

Red and white lights flickered. A crowd had gathered, gawking at the spectacle. Deputies kept the crowd at bay while the EMTs and paramedics worked to stabilize the perp. He had regained consciousness and was wailing in agony.

Paris Delaney arrived with her news crew, the camera lens soaking up the gory footage.

EMTs transferred the suspect onto a gurney, then loaded him into the back of the ambulance and closed the doors.

Mendoza approached us. "The suspect refused to tell the paramedics his name, but the ID in his wallet says Jarvis Jackson. I ran his record, and the punk's got a rap sheet as long as my dick."

JD deadpanned, "So, he's clean?"

Mendoza's eyes narrowed at him. "Multiple possession charges, burglary, shoplifting, grand theft auto. Did a nickel in Dade County."

"Known associates?" I asked.

"His co-conspirator in the prior auto theft was Grady McMorris."

"What do you say we go track down Grady, see what he has to say?" JD suggested with a grin.

"According to the records, Grady lives with his girlfriend at the Hogfish Palace Apartments in Jamaica Village."

"You got a mugshot on this guy?" I asked.

We followed Mendoza to his patrol car and pulled up Grady's information on the computer screen. I took one look at his mug shot. "Yep. That's our shooter."

"FYI, the owner of the vehicle didn't make it," Mendoza said.

I cringed.

"Where's his wife?" I asked.

"She's still at the scene, giving Erickson a full statement," Mendoza said.

"Tell Erickson to show her Grady's mugshot and get a positive ID. Between her statement and ours, that ought to be enough for a warrant."

Mendoza clicked his walkie talkie and spoke to Erickson.

"Incoming," JD muttered, nodding to Paris and her crew marching our way.

I groaned but put on a good front. Within seconds, the camera lens focused on us.

"Deputy Wild, what can you tell us about this unfortunate tragedy?"

"A carjacking resulted in the death of a vehicle owner. One suspect remains at large, and one is in custody."

"This is the second pursuit within a matter of days that has resulted in the critical injury of a suspect. What do you have to say about that?"

"Crime doesn't pay," I said dryly.

"Again, this is a situation that could have been avoided."

"I agree," I said to Paris's surprise. "These individuals made a choice to break the law today."

"Yes, but doesn't that speak to—"

"Do me a favor... Go interview the victim's wife. Her life was shattered today. You want a story to tell? Tell the victim's story."

My eyes blazed into her. This was just another headline for her—more grist for the mill. A dramatic sound bite to draw in viewers. There would be another story tomorrow, and one the day after that, and the day after that. This tragedy would soon be forgotten by everyone except those involved. Paris didn't act out of malice, just indifference. It was entertainment masquerading as news. That's all it was.

I stormed down the sidewalk, marching back to *Juicy Burger*.

JD hustled alongside me. "Piece of advice... There are two words that you need to say to her from now on. *No comment*. That's it. Don't get into these discussions. You're just feeding into her agenda. And the way they'll cut the footage together, you'll end up looking like the bad guy."

"I know," I said.

Forensic investigators swarmed the intersection near *Juicy Burger* when we arrived. The traffic was backed up and moving at a snail's pace. Deputies managed the flow.

Cameras flashed as a forensic photographer documented the scene, and Brenda hovered over the victim's body. His wife sat in Erickson's patrol car sobbing.

We left the somber scene and headed to the station. I filled out a report and made a sworn affidavit. We were able to get a warrant to arrest Grady McMorris and search his residence. We put together a tac team, suited up with protective gear, and headed to Jamaica Village.

Grady lived in a dingy yellow apartment complex on Roosevelt Street. A white picket fence surrounded the rectangular complex. There were six units downstairs and six units upstairs. Window-mounted AC units rattled, and small porches were full of plants, toys, and bicycles. Beat up cars parked on the street had suffered plenty of dents and dings from mishaps on the narrow avenue. There was no covered parking, so vehicles were exposed to the elements 24/7 which faded paint and cracked interiors.

It wasn't the greatest neighborhood in the world.

There was no sign of the pearl Lexus.

It had probably already been delivered to a chop shop or stored in a warehouse for later transport. It was a $50,000 car, but I'd be surprised if Grady got $1,500 for it. The real work would be pulling it apart, filing down the VIN numbers, and replacing them. If you didn't want to go through the trouble of chopping it up and rebuilding it with a salvage title, you could make a quick buck pulling the seats, taking off the rims, and parting the car out.

The apartment was registered to Elise Eubanks. Grady had listed the address with his parole officer.

Mendoza and Robinson took the rear. JD and I advanced the walkway with Faulkner and Erickson. I banged on the door of apartment 6B and shouted, "Coconut County! We have a warrant!"

As soon as I finished the words, Faulkner and Erickson heaved a battering ram against the door. Like a shot from a cannon, the door broke from its hinges. The doorframe splintered, and the damn thing fell into the foyer like a drawbridge lowering.

I tossed in a few flash-bang grenades. They clattered down the foyer and bounced into the living room.

*Pop!*

*Pop!*

We advanced into the apartment with our weapons in the firing position. We moved with tactical precision, clearing the corners, storming into the hazy living room. The TV was on, and there were empty beer cans on the coffee table along with a bong and a tray of dirt weed.

The door to the bedroom was closed. I heard muffled voices inside.

I hovered by the doorway and shouted, "Grady, let's not make this situation worse."

"Fuck you!"

"You've got nowhere to go. We can do this the easy way or the hard way."

"Eat shit, pig!"

"Hard way," I muttered to myself. "Get down on the ground and put your hands behind your head. We're coming in."

"You're gonna regret that!"

I twisted the door handle, but it was locked. I gave a nod to Faulkner and Erickson, who readied the battering ram. It would make short work of the cheap door made from compressed particle board.

"If you're armed, put your weapon down," I shouted.

"Come and take it, bitch!"

Just as Erickson and Faulkner were about to lay the hammer down, a flurry of bullets punched through the bedroom door. The rattle of the submachine gun filled the tiny apartment.

We all ducked for cover as bullets rocketed across the living room and smacked the drywall, sending plumes of gypsum into the air.

I glanced at the squad, assessing their condition.

They all gave me a nod. Fortunately, no one had been hit.

More gunfire erupted from the bedroom. This time, Grady blasted through the bedroom window at Robinson and Mendoza outside. The muffled sound of shattering glass seeped from the bedroom.

More gunfire erupted as the deputies fired back.

JD kicked open the bedroom door, and we swung our weapons inside.

Grady continued to spray molten lead through the window. He swung the barrel of his N9 in our direction, and we unloaded our magazines with fury.

The clatter of gunfire and flicker of muzzle flash filled the bedroom.

Smoke hazed the air.

Grady's girlfriend curled in the corner, screeching in horror as her boyfriend twitched and convulsed with bullet hits. Blood spattered the walls, and when Grady finally hit the ground, he must have had 30 bullet holes in his chest.

I had no doubt Grady was high on something.

His girlfriend sobbed and moaned in the corner. She screeched at us, "You motherfuckers!"

The sharp smell of gunpowder mixed with the tinny metallic scent of blood. Crimson pools flowed around Grady's body, soaking the carpet.

I could only imagine how the news would cover the event.

## 40

"You guys need to slow down," Brenda said when she arrived on the scene. "I can't keep up."

"Tell these people to quit doing stupid stuff," JD said.

She went to work, examining Grady's remains. The forensics team snapped photos and collected evidence.

Grady's girlfriend cried and wailed, continuing to hurl insults at us. The weed on the coffee table, and the meth-amphetamine in the bedroom, were enough to put her into custody. She sat on the couch with her hands cuffed behind her back, tears streaming down her cheeks.

"Where's the stolen vehicle?" I asked.

"I don't know nothing about no stolen vehicle," Elise said.

"Who is his car connection?" I asked.

"He doesn't have a car connection."

"You realize that Grady killed someone this afternoon?"

"He didn't kill nobody. He's been here all afternoon with me. The only people who killed anyone are you guys. And I hope you all rot in hell."

"Ma'am, there are multiple eyewitnesses that can identify Grady as the shooter."

"You didn't have any right to break into my apartment and kill him," she screeched.

This conversation wasn't going anywhere.

Mendoza escorted Elise out of the apartment and marched her down the walkway to a squad car. She cussed and screamed the entire way.

A large crowd of neighbors had gathered around, gawking. The deafening racket of the shootout was hard to ignore.

The street was lit up with emergency vehicles, flashing and flickering. It was no surprise to see Paris and her news crew.

I cringed as I stepped outside. Deputies kept her at bay along with the rest of the crowd. It didn't keep Paris from shouting at me as I passed. "Deputy Wild, were you involved in the shooting?"

I ignored her.

We headed back to the station, filled out after-action reports, and debriefed the sheriff in the conference room with Mendoza, Robinson, Faulkner, and Erickson.

"You mean to tell me all of you were involved in the shooting?" Daniels asked with a grim frown.

We all glanced around at each other sheepishly.

"We'll know exactly who was involved when the lab analyzes the ballistics," I said.

"But you all fired at the suspect?"

"He posed an imminent threat," Faulkner said.

"I'm short on manpower as it is." Daniels sighed. "You know the drill. Take the rest of the day off. All of you. See the head shrinker, and surrender your duty weapons."

It was a matter of standard protocol to be put on administrative leave pending the outcome of a full investigation. It usually meant a day off.

We headed back to *Diver Down* to grab a beer, unwind, and get something to eat.

"I heard about the carjacking and the shooting," Teagan said as we sat in the bar. "Is everyone okay?"

"Everyone except the two perps and the vehicle owner," JD said.

"News said one was in stable condition at the hospital," Teagan replied.

The teal-eyed beauty grabbed two longnecks from a tub of ice, snatched a bottle opener from her back pocket, twirled it like a gunslinger, and popped the tops with a hiss. She slid the sweaty bottles across the counter.

We both gulped down a refreshing mouthful.

The mood was somber, but we both tried to file it away as just another crappy situation. This stuff could eat you up if you let it.

Jack ordered chicken quesadillas, and I opted for a chicken sandwich. Teagan served our meal, and we chowed down.

After we ate, we took the boat out for the afternoon, fished, shot the breeze, and drank more. We stayed on the water past sunset, then returned to the marina. We caught a few fish, but nothing much to speak of.

We got cleaned up, went to Oyster Avenue for dinner, then hit a few bars and called it an early evening. Jack stayed aboard the *Avventura* just in case my assassin decided to pay another visit.

I set the motion detector on the security cam to be extra sensitive. It would buzz my phone anytime there was activity. Not foolproof, by any means, but it might provide a heads up if someone tried to board the boat in the middle of the night.

What it did was wake me up every time somebody walked down the dock. Fortunately, there wasn't any foot traffic after 3 AM.

I made it through the night unscathed and woke as the morning sun filtered in, carving shafts of light into the stateroom. I was just out of the shower when Denise called. I grabbed the phone from the nightstand.

"I think you're gonna like this," she said.

"After yesterday, I could use a little good news."

"The weapons used by the carjackers match the ballistics in the Sledge case," Denise said.

That took me by surprise. "Are you sure about that?"

"That's what the lab tells me. I called the hospital. Jarvis is stable and able to take visitors. I figured you guys might want to have a little chat with him."

"Indeed."

"The lab was able to pull several fingerprints from the weapons that match up with Grady and Jarvis. But that's not all."

I waited for her to continue.

"There was a partial print on the magazine that got a high-probability match in the database with a third person."

"With whom?"

## 41

"**A** guy named Marcus Irvin," Denise said.

"That's Kane's #1 guy," I replied.

"I'm still waiting on Sledge's toxicology report. There's some hang-up at the lab. I'll let you know when that comes through."

"Thank you!"

I ended the call and rousted JD out of bed. After breakfast, we went to the hospital and found Jarvis in an intermediate care unit. He was in a cast that went from his thigh all the way down to his ankle. His left arm was also in a cast from the wrist to the elbow. His head was bandaged, and his face was black and blue.

Jarvis wasn't too pleased to see us, and neither were the visitors in his room. His eyes rounded when he saw me and JD. "Oh, hell no! I ain't talking to you."

"You're in a lot of trouble, Jarvis," I said.

"He's not saying anything without a lawyer," his mother chimed in. She sat next to his girlfriend.

Both of them glared at us.

"Okay," I said. "Fine by me. But just so you know, the weapons you two used in the carjacking were also used in the murder of MC Sledge."

Jarvis's eyes widened. "What!?"

"I'm sure you're aware that your partner is dead," I said.

Jarvis said nothing, but a grim frown tensed his face.

"You motherfuckers killed him."

"He'd still be alive if he surrendered," I said.

"Jarvis, keep your mouth shut," his mother said.

"Right now, you're looking at accessory to murder in the carjacking case and first-degree murder in the killing of MC Sledge," I said.

Anger built on his face. He tried to bite his tongue but finally blurted out, "I didn't kill anybody. How was I supposed to know the driver had a gun and Grady would have to shoot him?"

"Grady didn't have to shoot anybody. And you two didn't have to steal the car," I said. "What did you think was gonna happen when you jacked the vehicle?"

"I thought it would go down just like every other time we did it." His eyes widened again as the words slipped out of his mouth.

"Goddammit, Jarvis!" his mother snapped. "I told you to keep that dumb mouth of yours shut."

Jarvis's face crinkled. He hesitated a moment, then spoke. *Some people just can't help themselves.* "The guns were just for show. I didn't count on anybody dying. And I certainly didn't kill MC Sledge. I love that cat's music."

I gave him a stern gaze.

"The guns weren't mine," Jarvis said. "I swear. They were Grady's."

I took everything he said with a grain of salt. "Where did he get them from?"

Jarvis shrugged.

His mother scolded him. "What part of *shut up* do you not understand?"

His face twisted. "It ain't gonna make any difference now."

"Where did you get the guns?" I asked again.

"I don't know where Grady got them."

My eyes narrowed at him. "What's your affiliation with Dragon Nation?"

"Who?"

"Cut the crap!"

"Jarvis..." his mother cautioned.

Jarvis was silent for a long moment.

"We're trying to help your son, ma'am," I said.

"You're trying to help him into a life sentence," she said.

"If he cooperates, he could receive a lesser sentence," I said.

"There's a big *if* in that statement," Jarvis's mother said.

I asked Jarvis once again, "Where did you get the guns?"

He was silent for a long moment. His eyes flicked between his mother and me. She gave him another stern gaze. Then his eyes darted back to mine. "What kind of deal can you give me?"

"I'll talk to the DA. I'll put in a good word and say you were cooperative. Maybe you can walk away from this thing with an involuntary manslaughter charge."

"How long would I have to serve?"

I shrugged. "That would take the death penalty off the table."

His eyes widened again. "The death penalty?"

"That's what happens when you get convicted in a capital murder case. The death penalty is always a possibility."

"I'm telling you, I didn't kill nobody."

"Then start talking."

Jarvis was silent for a long moment. Resigned to his fate, he let out a sigh. "Okay. We, I mean, Grady," he said, quickly correcting himself, "got the weapons from a guy named Marcus."

"Marcus Irvin?"

"If you knew, why did you ask me?"

"When did you get them?"

"Day before yesterday, I think. That bastard said they were clean too. I didn't know they'd been used to kill Sledge."

"I need you to make a sworn affidavit."

"A what?"

"A signed statement to what you just told me."

## 42

With Jarvis's statement and the print on the N9 magazine, we were able to get an arrest warrant for Marcus Irvin. We found him aboard Kane's yacht.

The tac-team stormed across the passerelle in full gear, weapons shouldered.

As we hit the aft deck, I shouted, "Coconut County! We have a warrant."

Mendoza and Robinson advanced along the starboard side passageway, while Deputies Albright and Flanagan took the port side.

We hung back with Erickson and Faulkner. I pulled open the salon door, and we stormed inside.

Marcus emerged from a forward passageway with a confused look on his face. "What the hell is going on?"

"On the ground!" I shouted. "Now!"

Marcus raised his hands in the air, then knelt down and ate the deck.

We kept our weapons aimed at the perp while Faulkner and Erickson rushed forward and slapped the cuffs around his meaty wrists. They yanked him to his feet and dragged him toward the stern, reading him his rights.

Mendoza and Robinson had found Kane on the foredeck. They escorted him to the salon. He wasn't in custody. At this point, we had nothing on him. I hoped that was about to change.

"Can someone tell me what's happening?" Kane asked.

"Your right-hand man is under arrest for the murder of Sheldon Livingston," I said.

He scoffed. "That's ridiculous. What evidence do you have?"

"Oh, just the murder weapon with his fingerprints on it," I snarked.

Kane kept a stone face.

"I can assure you, Marcus is 100% innocent of any charges."

"We're gonna get you next," I assured.

"Is that a threat, Deputy?"

"Just a statement of fact."

"It seems like you have developed a personal vendetta. I have a mind to sue the department for targeted harassment."

"Funny. I hear that a lot. It never works out too well."

Marcus was taken back to the station, processed, printed, and thrown into an interrogation room. We let him sit a while before getting down to business. When JD and I finally entered the small room, we took a seat across the table from him.

I placed the murder weapon and the magazine in an evidence bag on the table in front of him. The gun wasn't loaded, and Marcus's wrists were cuffed and chained at his waist. His ankles were restrained.

"I hope you like orange," I said. "You're going to be wearing it for a while."

The big ogre just stared at me.

"Recognize that gun?"

He looked at it for a brief second. "What about it?"

I was relieved that he decided to talk. I figured he might just shut the hell up. "Your fingerprint was found on the magazine."

"So?"

"That weapon was used to kill Sheldon Livingston."

"So?"

"I'm sure you can see where I'm going with this."

He glared at me, hunched in his seat, his head disappearing into his thick neck.

"That connects you to the murder weapon. I've got a sworn affidavit from a person who says the gun was purchased from you the day before yesterday. It's not looking good for you."

"Proves nothing."

"It proves that at some point in time, you handled the weapon."

"No, it proves at some point I handled the magazine. Big difference."

"The two often go hand-in-hand."

"Sounds like the seeds of reasonable doubt to me," Marcus said with a faint grin. "Is this all you've got?"

I didn't like his smug grin. "Those weapons were converted to full automatic fire."

"I sold some punk kids a couple of *legal* magazines. That's it."

"As I mentioned, I have a sworn affidavit."

"A sworn affidavit from a crackhead. Is that what you based this arrest on? Good luck with that. I was never in possession of those weapons."

My face tensed.

"I didn't kill Sledge. And you can't put me at the scene."

"We know Kane ordered the hit," I said. We didn't know anything for sure. "Cooperate, and maybe you can get a lesser charge."

"You don't know shit. You've concocted this theory in your mind, and it's nothing more than fantasy."

This guy was getting on my nerves.

A cocky smirk tugged his lips. "Does this tactic actually work with some people?"

## 43

Marcus's personal belongings were confiscated when he was processed. I had his cell phone in my pocket but couldn't get past the lock screen. I pulled the device from my pocket and held it in front of Marcus's face. "Recognize this?"

His face twisted. "That's my phone."

The screen unlocked, and I began to scroll through his messages.

"You can't search my phone!"

"Yes, I can. The courts have ruled that biometric information can be compelled. Should have used a passcode instead. That's protected under the 4th Amendment."

Marcus growled at us.

He'd been using an encrypted messaging app for most of his communications, and the messages were set to disappear after a certain time. Unfortunately, I couldn't find any communication between him and Kane that was incriminating. But I did find some un-encrypted text messages that were interesting.

"Who's Kehlani?" I asked. "Girlfriend?"

Marcus's face tightened.

I scrolled through the messages. There were some steamy texts between the two and some provocative photos. I recognized the girl. I lifted an impressed eyebrow. "Attractive."

I showed JD the naughty pictures. He was equally impressed. I did it just to get under Marcus's skin.

"That's one of Kane's girls, isn't it?"

Marcus's face tensed.

"How do you think he'd feel about you having a little tryst with one of his concubines?"

"You have no right to look through my shit," Marcus snapped.

"Seems like we do. I wonder what else I'm gonna find on this phone?" I pushed away from the table and stood up.

JD followed me to the door.

"Are you sure there's nothing more you want to tell me about Kane?" I asked. "I'm gonna give this phone to our tech guys, and they'll be able to pull all kinds of information from the device. They'll make a clone of the drive, and they might even be able to resurrect deleted files and messages."

Concern tensed Marcus's face.

I waited for a moment, but he said nothing.

"Enjoy your night in jail."

"That's all it's going to be," he said. "I'm out tomorrow. You watch."

I knocked on the door, and the guard buzzed us out of the interrogation room. We stepped into the hallway.

I kept scrolling through the phone so the screen wouldn't lock out. I pulled my phone from my pocket and called Isabella. "I need you to text spyware to a target phone."

"What do you need to accomplish?" she asked.

"I need to be able to track the device and activate the microphone remotely without letting the user know about it."

"I've got just the app for you."

I gave her Marcus's phone number.

"I'm going to send a text message. Just click the link, and the app will self-install. Delete the message after installation. The app will run in the background, and he will never know it's there unless he runs sweeper software on his phone. Even then, this stuff is so new there's a good chance the sweeper would miss it."

An instant later, the text buzzed on Marcus's phone. I clicked the link. It seemed like nothing had happened.

"Is that it?" I asked. "Did it work?"

"Hang on a second," Isabella said. After a brief pause, she continued, "Yup. Give me a mic check."

"Testing, one, two, three..."

"Coming through loud and clear," Isabella said.

I deleted the text message containing the link on Marcus's phone. "Is there a way I can monitor this from my phone?"

"Absolutely. I'll send you a download link for the monitoring app."

"You're not gonna start spying on me now, are you?"

"Would I do such a thing?" she replied in a sly voice.

"You know everything anyway."

"That I do."

She sent the link, and I installed the monitoring app. It looked like any other. I tapped the icon to launch it. It was pretty handy. The interface allowed you to enter multiple numbers, which you could monitor. I clicked the plus icon and added Marcus's phone number. Once it was entered into the interface, all I had to do was click on the number, and I had complete control of the microphone and a real-time feed of the GPS tracking information.

I verified that everything was working on my end, then thanked Isabella and ended the call.

JD smiled. "Ain't technology great?"

I had no doubt that Marcus would make bail after his arraignment. Kane would put it up. I knew the gangster didn't want his right-hand man sitting in lock-up, getting funny ideas about turning State's evidence.

With surveillance capabilities in place, all I had to do was go to the judge and get a warrant for the wiretap. I'd leave out the minor detail that I had already installed the spyware.

I gave the device to the nerd herd. They copied the drive before putting the phone with the rest of Marcus's personal belongings. The spyware had a keylogger that would record and upload every keystroke, including passcodes. It would come in handy if we ever needed to access the cloned drive.

There was no doubt in my mind that Kane and his crew were responsible for Sledge's death. The infamous rapper may have been of dubious moral character, but I was determined to bring Kane and company down.

JD was eager to point out that it was almost happy hour, so we set out to do our part in supporting local businesses.

"You seemed to do so well at Jellyfish the other night. I'm thinking we should go back," Jack teased.

My eyes narrowed at him. "Anyplace but Jellyfish."

"But that's the last place your assassin will look for you."

He had a point.

I entered Jellyfish with trepidation, scanning the club for any sign of the deadly vixen. I knew she wouldn't be there, but I had an unsettling feeling nonetheless. It was like revisiting the scene of a bad accident.

It was pretty tame. Jellyfish didn't heat up until later. The crowd was thin at this point. We downed a couple drinks, then grabbed something to eat at *Blowfish*. Afterward, we met the rest of the band at *Mutiny* to watch Faye's band, *Lip Bomb,* perform. They didn't go on until 10:30 PM. They played an hour-long set. Afterward, we all hung out and drank more than we should have.

Faye's band was warming up to us. But their lead singer was still concerned we would steal her permanently.

The guys wanted to bring the party back to the boat, but I cautioned them that since somebody was still trying to kill me, it might not be a good idea.

"There's safety in numbers," Crash said. "Anybody messes with you, they gotta go through us first."

I chuckled, appreciative of the sentiment. But Crash had no idea what he was getting into. His mouth was certainly writing big checks.

If I were Sophia Breslin, I'd wait a while, let my target relax and forget about the threat. Then I'd strike. But impatient employers often demand immediate results. Still, I wasn't too concerned about an attack this evening.

There was no stopping the forward momentum of the after-party. We all wound up on the *Avventura* for a late-night soirée. *Wild Fury's* sudden and meteoric rise had turned them into local celebrities, and the band attracted a growing bevy of beauties—many of whom were eager to ditch their skimpy attire and frolic naked in the Jacuzzi aboard the boat.

Being the manager of the band certainly came with its share of perks.

Daniels called bright and early the next morning. I grabbed the phone from the nightstand and peeled open my eyes, feeling a little wrecked from the previous night's indulgences.

"You want the good news or the bad news first?"

## 44

"**B**ad news—Marcus is processing out," Daniels said. "DA declined to bring charges. Not enough evidence."

I groaned.

"Good news—judge approved the wiretap. Stay on the bastard and see what you can find out."

"I'm on it."

I ended the call and pulled myself out of bed. After I hit the head and brushed my teeth, I headed down to the main deck and banged on the hatch to JD's stateroom. "Get your ass up! Marcus is getting sprung. We gotta roll."

I heard signs of life, so I went to the galley, put on a pot of coffee, and started breakfast.

The boat wasn't in bad shape. A few empty beer bottles and glasses here and there. Our impromptu party wasn't too big, not like after a show.

Crash stumbled up to the main deck from the guest quarters. He took a seat at the settee just off the galley. He had a glum look on his face.

"You're up early," I said.

"Couldn't sleep."

"Want some coffee?"

"Yeah. Might as well get wired up."

"Something bothering you?"

"No. I don't think so." He paused. "I mean, yeah. Sort of."

"You take cream and sugar?"

"Load it up."

I poured a cup and mixed in generous helpings of the good stuff, then delivered it.

"Thanks, bro."

"So what gives?" I asked, slipping into the seat across from him.

He sighed, then glanced around to make sure no one was coming. "I'm so totally screwed."

I tensed with dread. "What did you do? Don't tell me you did something illegal?"

"No. Nothing illegal." He hesitated. "It's stupid."

"Out with it."

He shook his head. "Naw, man. Forget it. It's not a big deal."

"I'm your manager. This is what I'm here for. If you've got a problem, let's nip it in the bud."

He paused for a long moment, then gave another look around. "I think I love her, dude."

I sighed. I don't know if I was relieved that it wasn't something worse or concerned about the implications for the band.

"I know, dude. It's bad. It just happened."

"It always does."

"I know we're just supposed to be hooking up, but... I don't know what it is, man. I just can't get enough."

"How does she feel?"

Crash shrugged. "I don't think she wants anything complicated. She likes her freedom."

"Have you talked to her about this?"

"No. I don't want to mess things up."

"I'm probably the last person you need to take relationship advice from, but life is too short to play games. I'd lay it on the table. If she's not buying what you're selling, move on."

He frowned. "That sounds good in theory, but it's the moving on part that makes me nervous."

"Just don't let it affect your relationship with the rest of the guys."

He nodded. "I won't. I mean, I know she hooked up with JD. But that was before we hooked up, so it doesn't really bother me. As long as he doesn't go back there."

"He knows she's off-limits now. It doesn't take a rocket scientist to see that you've got more than a casual interest in her."

Crash was such a genuine, kind-hearted guy. He may have been a little rough around the edges, but he'd be there for his friends in a heartbeat. I didn't want to see him get heartbroken.

"Losing sleep over it isn't going to change the outcome. Life has a funny way of working itself out all on its own. I know you're head over heels right now. She elevates your pulse and makes you feel nervous inside. When you're with her, it feels like anything is possible, and when you're apart, it seems like the end of the world."

He nodded.

"But the person you're supposed to be with will see you for who you are and appreciate that. It may be Faye. It may be somebody else."

"It's the *somebody else* part that I don't want to think about."

"Either way, you gotta keep your chin up, be true to yourself, and have faith that good things are ahead."

"Thanks, Tyson. You're a good friend."

"Anytime."

"You can't tell anybody."

"Tell anybody what?" JD asked as he stumbled into the galley, wiping the sleep from his eyes. He went straight toward the coffee maker and poured a cup.

Crash tensed.

I changed the subject. "We gotta hurry up and get out of here."

"Slow your roll," JD said. He looked at his watch. "You know how long it takes to process out of the system."

I moved back to the stovetop, took the bacon out of the pan, and dished up the eggs. We all took a seat at the settee and chowed down.

After breakfast, JD and I headed over to the detention center and waited for Marcus to be released. We parked at the curb a block away. When he strolled out of the facility, I launched the surveillance app on my phone and began monitoring him.

The app would record MP3 files while activated. The only downside to the app was that it drew power from the target device, causing reduced battery life. The drain could cause Marcus to become suspicious if he needed to recharge his phone more frequently than normal.

Omar, one of Kane's goons, picked him up in a white SUV. I couldn't quite see through the tinted windows, but I could make out the silhouette of a figure in the backseat. I thought it might be Kane.

Marcus hopped into the passenger seat, and we followed the SUV back to the marina at *Pelican Point*.

"You look like shit," Omar said, his voice crackling through the speaker in my phone.

Road and engine noise cluttered the signal. Marcus's cell phone was in his pocket, which further muffled the sound.

"That place sucks," Marcus replied.

"The food is fucking terrible in there, isn't it?" Omar said.

"They asked about the guns, right?" Kane asked.

"They don't have shit on me," Marcus assured.

"They have a fingerprint on a magazine."

"If they had something, I wouldn't be sitting in this car right now."

"Did they offer you a deal?" Kane asked.

"Of course. They wanted me to roll over."

"Maybe that's why no charges were brought," Kane said in a subtle but ominous tone.

## 45

"I t's disappointing," Kane said. "When I ask that something be done, I expect it to be done quickly and efficiently."

"I'm sorry," Marcus said. "It's my fault. I messed up."

"I asked you specifically to—"

Static crackled over the line, and the conversation dropped out.

My face tensed.

The SUV turned into the marina, and the driver pulled up to the dock. Kane and Marcus hopped out of the vehicle, and Omar continued on to a parking space.

The two thugs ambled down the dock toward the *Scrilla*.

JD and I continued past the marina, trying not to look like an obvious tail. A Miami Blue Porsche drew a lot of unwanted attention at times.

The cell signal picked up again.

"Look, there's nothing to worry about," Marcus assured. "If it comes down to it, it's all on me."

We circled back around and pulled into the parking lot. JD looked for a space.

I kept my eye on the dock, watching the two goons stroll toward the *Scrilla*. Omar caught up with them.

"Let me see your phone," Kane said to Marcus.

He dug into his pocket and handed him the device.

"Did they get access?" Kane asked.

Marcus hesitated. "Sort of. But they didn't find anything. I don't keep sensitive shit on the phone. I delete all messages."

The conversation was a lot clearer now, but the wind whipped across the microphone, causing added noise.

Kane tossed the phone into the water, and the signal went dead.

My jaw clenched tight, and an obscenity may have slipped from my lips.

"So much for that plan," JD muttered. "What now?"

I shrugged.

"If I were Marcus, I'd be a little nervous at this point in time. Kane's wondering if he ratted him out."

I watched the goons board the *Scrilla*. Omar disconnected shore power and water and cast off the lines.

"Let's head back to the marina," JD said. "We'll take the wake boat and follow them."

JD pulled out of the lot, and we zipped back to *Diver Down*. We hopped out of the car and sprinted down the dock. I grabbed a couple fishing poles from the *Avventura*, along with binoculars, night vision opticals (in case we were out late), assault rifles, extra magazines, a couple sodas, and snacks for a stakeout.

We loaded the gear into the wake boat, and JD cast off the lines. I cranked up the engine and idled out of the marina. After the breakwater, I throttled up, bringing the boat on plane.

We hustled around the island, spitting a frothy wake, heading toward *Pelican Point*. We were quicker and more nimble than Kane's superyacht, and we had gotten over to the marina just after they had cleared the breakwater.

We hung back and followed them as they cruised out to sea, keeping a reasonable distance.

I was concerned that Marcus might end up at the bottom of the ocean with a pair of cement shoes, or at least an anchor tied around his waist. One less thug in the world wouldn't necessarily be a bad thing. But I wasn't keen on letting Kane get away with murder. And right now, Marcus was our only connection to the crime.

We followed them for almost an hour. They finally dropped anchor just north of Barracuda Key.

I watched through binoculars as we pretended to fish.

Kane and Marcus were on the aft deck of the *Scrilla*, laughing and smiling. It seemed like they were getting along well. Kane could have been putting on a good front. I fully expected him to put a bullet in Marcus and shove him over-board, but it never happened.

Kane stepped into the salon and emerged a moment later with a black duffel bag. He and Marcus launched a tender, climbed aboard with Omar, and cranked up the small outboard engine. They sped away from the *Scrilla* and cruised in with the surf to the north shore of Barracuda Key. They ran the tender up to the beach.

Marcus hopped out of the rigid inflatable and pulled the boat onto the sand. The trio marched into the underbrush, the duffel bag dangling from Kane's hand.

It looked mighty suspicious.

With binoculars, I scanned the horizon. I saw a craft fast approaching from the south—a *Go-Fast* boat kicking up a rooster tail.

The sun glimmered on the water. I watched the Go-Fast boat cruise to the south shore. They anchored in the surf, and two goons hopped out with a duffel bag of their own and proceeded to the tree line.

It didn't take a rocket scientist to figure out what was about to go down.

"Do we sit back and let this thing play out, or do we go spoil the party?" I asked.

JD shrugged. "They'll hear us coming."

"Bring us a little closer," I said.

JD climbed behind the wheel, cranked up the engines, and headed toward Barracuda Key.

I called Sheriff Daniels and told him a drug deal was going down. I told him to send the Coast Guard. They'd be able to board the *Scrilla* and search the vessel after the transaction had taken place. Hopefully, we'd catch Kane with a duffel bag of drugs.

As we approached the island, the clatter of gunfire rang out.

It was impossible to see through the forest on the island, but I caught glimpses of muzzle flash through the trees. The firefight lasted less than a minute. I knew from experience that a minute could seem like an eternity when you were in the middle of it.

I heard the rumble of another boat approaching. My eyes scanned the horizon, but I didn't see the craft. It was on the other side of the island.

A moment later, a two-man fire team emerged from the tree line on the west shore—each hauling a duffel bag. They had assault rifles and were decked out in Coast Guard uniforms.

Our pirates had moved up the food chain. Instead of knocking off wealthy yacht owners, they were robbing drug dealers. Something that was more lucrative and dangerous.

The sound of outboards drew closer. What appeared to be a Coast Guard patrol boat rounded the island and pulled to the west shore. The pirates hefted the duffel bags into the boat, then climbed aboard. The driver banked the vehicle around and throttled up. The engines howled, spitting whitewater.

JD throttled up and gave chase.

These were the same pirates. I was sure of it. How many marauders could there be masquerading as the Coast Guard?

But the four-man team was now down to three—the driver of the boat and the two-man team.

The wake boat bounced across the surface of the water, crashing against the swells, spraying mists of saltwater. JD had the throttle at full.

I grabbed an AR 15 and crouched at the bow—the wind blasting my face as we charged forward.

The fake patrol boat was fast, but our little wake boat had some get up and go, and we were slowly gaining on the pirate craft. It didn't take long for them to notice. One of the pirates shouldered his rifle, leaned against the stern, and squeezed off several rounds in our direction. Muzzle flash flickered, and bullets snapped across the bow.

JD zigzagged, making us a more difficult target.

We were on our own. It would take a while for the real Coast Guard to get here. The pirates had a hell of a lot more firepower than we did. And we were about to find out just how much.

## 46

More bullets rifled in our direction.

JD crouched low behind the helm station while I huddled behind the gunwale. I fired a few shots back at the pirates for good measure. We were about 60 yards behind them. With the bouncing swells at this distance, it was just harassment fire. Nobody was going to hit anything unless they were extremely lucky.

We kept inching closer to the pirate craft. Pretty soon, we were 50 yards behind them. I guess that was too close for comfort. One of the pirates reached to the deck, snatched a tubular device, and shouldered an RPG-7.

My eyes rounded at the sight.

JD saw it too.

The rocket launcher was a Soviet designed anti-tank weapon. Rugged, cheap, and effective, the RPG-7 is the most popular grenade launcher in the world. It's been in continuous use since the Vietnam era. It can fire a variety of anti-armor or anti-personnel warheads. Simple, reliable, and relatively accurate. Each warhead is equipped with a safety cap that protects the impact fuse from unwanted detonations—when used properly.

The pirate unscrewed the safety cap, took aim at our boat, and squeezed the trigger.

The booster fired, and the grenade launched from the tube.

JD swerved the boat hard as a rocket ripped through the air.

It smacked the water on the port side, which was enough to trip the impact fuse on the nose of the warhead. The grenade exploded, shooting a geyser of water into the air.

The blast rocked the wake boat, lifting the port side hull out of the water. I thought we were going to flip over for a second, but we smacked back down and continued on the roller coaster through the swells.

My heart leaped into my throat.

JD angled the boat back on course, and we continued our pursuit. *It was probably a stupid thing to do.*

The pirate grabbed another rocket, slammed it into the tube, removed the safety cap, and took aim.

I squeezed the trigger, my rifle hammering against my shoulder. Flames flickered from the barrel, and I caught whiffs of gunpowder as we raced through the chop.

Another grenade rocketed in our direction. It zipped across the bow, clearing the boat by a few feet, then smacked into the swells.

Another explosion sent plumes of water into the sky.

The pirate reloaded, unscrewed the safety cap, and took aim.

I kept firing at the bastard, the deafening report echoing across the water. I unloaded the entire magazine in his direction as we bounced on the swells.

One of my bullets clipped his shoulder, spinning him around, tumbling him to the deck. The RPG nosed down. When the pirate fell, the nose of the grenade hit the deck, tripping the impact fuse.

I can't tell you the number of morons I've seen in Afghan combat zones running around with safety caps removed from RPG-7s, despite the number of times they were advised not to. All it takes is an inconvenient stumble.

The device detonated, and the fake patrol boat exploded, spidering debris in all directions. Bits of metal, body parts, blood, and guts spewed out. A plume of smoke expanded. The duffel bags full of cocaine and cash dispersed. A couple million dollars fluttered on the breeze like a ticker-tape parade, and a mist of cocaine hung in the air.

I stared at the spectacle with wide eyes and exchanged a glance with an equally stunned JD.

"Holy shit!" he muttered.

We circled the debris field as bills fluttered to the surface of the water—some of them charred, others seemingly intact.

The smoke cloud dissipated with the breeze. There wasn't much left of the boat or its occupants. There was nothing to salvage or rescue except for the money.

Not one to let it go to waste, JD grabbed a net and tried to scoop up as much money as he could. He had to act fast before it got saturated and sank.

He managed to get about $10,000 into the boat while the majority of it either drifted away or sank. He made a note of the GPS position so we could come back out and dive for it later. There was no telling how far the current would carry it.

We headed back to Barracuda Key and anchored in the surf near the south shore, not far from the drug dealer's Go-Fast boat. We hopped out with our weapons drawn and advanced through the underbrush. I heard the distant sound of a helicopter approaching. The rotor blades pattered, and I figured it was probably the Coast Guard. The *real* Coast Guard.

We reached the clearing in the center of the island and saw the carnage. Kane, Marcus, and Omar were dead—their bodies riddled with bullet holes. The same for the two thugs that had arrived in the *Go-Fast* boat—Kane's drug connection.

Near the tree line lay one of the pirates dressed in a Coast Guard uniform. He had taken a bullet to the neck. Needless to say, he wasn't breathing anymore.

I figured the marauders had been casing Kane and his group for weeks, and they picked up on the regular exchange point. Maybe they had intercepted Kane's communications. Maybe one of Kane's beauties was a spy, relaying information to the pirates. It didn't matter how they got the intel, they had been waiting in ambush on the island. It would have been a nice score for them.

The Coast Guard helicopter thumped overhead. I flashed my badge and waved.

Soon, the island was overrun with deputies and first responders. The forensics team snapped photos, and Brenda evaluated the bodies. The Coast Guard boarded Kane's boat and searched it. There were a few bikini-clad beauties on board. They were all taken into custody and brought back to the station where they'd be questioned and most likely released —uninvolved bystanders, but perhaps not entirely innocent.

We wrapped up on the island and headed back to Coconut Key. We filled out after-action reports, and I convinced JD to report the recovered drug money. It wasn't like he needed it.

Kane and Marcus had gotten their due, but I lacked the satisfaction of bringing them to justice myself. There was no doubt in my mind they were responsible for Sledge's death.

I got thrown for a loop when Denise poked her head into the conference room.

"Sheldon Livingston's toxicology report finally came back from the lab," she said. "This case is far from over."

## 47

"**S**heldon Livingston would have died whether somebody shot him or not," Denise said.

I lifted a curious brow.

"There was enough ethylene glycol in his system to kill him that night."

"Antifreeze?"

Denise nodded. "Somebody could have put it in his food or drink. I heard about one lady who even made pudding with this stuff and fed it to her husband."

"Good to know," JD said.

"Looks like somebody else was trying to kill him besides Kane and Marcus."

"It would have to be somebody with access," I said.

"Lucas," JD said with conviction.

"He was alone on the island with Sledge that night," I said. "He's been living there. He had access."

"I think we need to go back to Starfish Key and have a look around," JD said.

"I think you're right."

"I'll see if I can pull credit card receipts," Denise said. "See if Lucas purchased antifreeze recently."

We got a warrant to search the property at Starfish Key. We headed out there with a forensics team and took a county patrol boat.

We tied up at the dock and made our way down the passage toward the house. The sun was dipping down beyond the horizon by the time we arrived. We moved around the pool, and I banged on the studio door.

Lucas pulled it open a few minutes later. He looked surprised to see us. "Deputy Wild, to what do I owe the pleasure?"

"We have a warrant to search the premises."

His face crinkled. "What for?"

"You don't happen to have any antifreeze around, do you?"

He looked like he had seen a ghost.

"No. I mean, Sledge might have some."

We pushed into the studio and looked around. I snapped on a pair of nitrile gloves, pulled an empty liquor bottle from a trash can, and put it in an evidence bag.

"What are you doing with that?"

"Going to test for residue and fingerprints."

Lucas swallowed hard.

JD took the stairs up to Lucas's loft.

"Why are you looking in my private space?"

"We have a warrant that says we can search the entire premises," I said.

Concern bathed Lucas's face.

We looked around the loft, collecting all the liquor bottles we found. Some were full, some were empty.

"You guys are taking my entire stash," Lucas complained.

"I don't think you'll be needing it anymore."

We logged each item and documented where it came from.

I looked in the trash cans, and JD searched the closet. "Got something!"

JD held up a plastic container of antifreeze that was half empty.

Lucas's body stiffened.

"I thought you said you didn't have any antifreeze," I said.

"I don't know how that got in there."

"You're under arrest for the attempted murder of Sheldon Livingston."

He protested as I slapped the cuffs around his wrists. "What are you talking about? He was shot."

"He was poisoned, and he would have died."

I escorted him downstairs and back to the patrol boat while the rest of the forensics investigators searched the main house and Sheldon's yacht. They found more bottles of liquor aboard.

"Why did you kill your best friend?" I asked.

"I didn't kill anybody," Lucas said.

I shook my head. "Let me tell you how this is gonna play out. We're gonna get your credit card and phone records. I'll bet you money there's an antifreeze purchase on there. It's gonna correlate with the antifreeze we found in your closet. Because, you know, everybody keeps antifreeze in their closet," I said dryly. "We are also gonna find residue in one of those whiskey bottles. We're gonna find your fingerprints on the bottle. It won't take a lot of convincing to get a jury to think you attempted to kill Sheldon."

"But he died from gunshots. What does it matter now?"

"Oh, it matters," I said. "And the courts here in Florida prosecute attempted murder the same as a murder charge. Since you clearly planned this out, you are looking at a minimum of 25 years."

Lucas swallowed hard. He hesitated for a long moment, sweat sprouting on his forehead. "It wasn't my idea."

"I'm listening."

"I didn't have nothing to do with it. It was all Talia."

"Did she poison the whiskey, or did she tell you to do it?"

He hesitated for a long moment. "She told me to do it. But I didn't have a choice."

"Oh really?"

"Yeah. I had no control. I was temporarily insane."

"Temporarily insane?"

"The girl has got some good..." He grunted lewdly. "I fell in love. I must have lost my mind."

I sighed and shook my head. "So, you planned to kill your best friend so you could be with his wife?"

"Soon to be ex-wife." He paused. Then cringed, admitting, "That's pretty bad, isn't it?"

I nodded.

He let out a solemn exhale, and his body slumped. He hung his head and teared up. "Man, I'm a shitty friend. You know, when Sledge got shot, I felt relieved. I felt like, *thank God*, you know... I didn't kill him."

"He would have died anyway," I said.

"I don't know what I was thinking."

"Clearly, you weren't."

"What happens now?"

"We go down to the station, you make a sworn statement, and we arrest Talia."

"You cut me a break if I cooperate?"

"Maybe the DA drops it down to 2nd degree. 15 years."

Lucas frowned. "15 is better than 25." He paused for a long moment. "You know, I almost feel better now. That shit was weighing heavy on me."

## 48

We headed to the *Trident Towers*, arrest warrant in hand. We banged on the door to Talia Livingston's condo.

We must have caught her as she was heading out for the evening. She was dressed to the nines—skimpy black dress that hugged her petite form, stiletto heels, and moisturized thighs. Damn nice ones at that. Her makeup was done to perfection with long lashes and smoky eye shadow. Her lips were plump and juicy.

She looked stunned when she opened the door. She caught her breath and forced a smile. "Deputies, I wish I would have known you were coming. I don't have time to talk right now. I've got an appointment."

"I'm sorry, but you'll need to cancel."

Her face twisted with confusion. "Excuse me?"

"You're under arrest for the attempted murder of your husband."

Her jaw went slack.

"What are you talking about? I didn't shoot him."

"Put your hands behind your head and turn around."

"You can't arrest me! This is preposterous!"

"We know about the antifreeze. We have a sworn statement from a co-conspirator."

Her face crinkled. "What!?"

"Turn around. Now. Put your hands behind your head."

She complied.

I grabbed her delicate wrist and wrenched her arm behind her back. I slapped the cuffs on, then grabbed her other hand and locked her up.

"Ouch," she whined.

"Get used to it," I said. "You have the right to remain silent..."

I pulled her out of the apartment and escorted her down the hallway.

"Would you please close and lock my door, so all of my shit isn't stolen when I come back?"

"You're not coming back," I said.

JD did as she asked, then caught up with us.

I pressed the call button to the elevator and waited for the lift to arrive. "How long have you been having an affair with Lucas?"

Her eyes flicked to me, seething. "I want to speak with an attorney."

"Suit yourself."

The bell rang, and the elevator doors slid open. We stepped on board and plummeted down to the lobby.

Talia looked embarrassed. Her cheeks reddened as we dragged her toward the exit, past the concierge and gawking residents.

Erickson and Faulkner waited with a patrol car underneath the awning. Faulkner grabbed the door, and I stuffed Talia into the backseat. "Watch your head."

She glared at me again, and Faulkner closed the door.

"I'm impressed," he said. "You two handled her all by yourselves, and nobody died."

"There's a first time for everything," I replied.

Talia was processed, printed, and put into the holding pod. She was a lot smarter than Lucas and wasn't about to say anything.

I had her cellmate pulled from the housing pod, and I proposed a deal. She was in for possession of methamphetamine and armed robbery. She was still awaiting trial. I told her I'd put $50 in her commissary if she could get Talia to talk and confess to the murder. It's amazing what people will tell their cellmates, either out of boredom or the need to get it off their chest. It's often their undoing.

We filled out after-action reports, then headed to *Tide Pool* for a drink. It had been an interesting day, and I was glad to have these cases behind us.

JD insisted I buy all the drinks since I made him fork over the recovered cash.

There was still the pesky matter of that hired assassin and her employer. I was sure somebody would come for me sooner or later.

I'd be ready and waiting.

*Ready for more?*
*The adventure continues with Wild Secret!*

## DON'T MISS THE ADVENTURE

*Join my newsletter and find out what happens next!*

## AUTHOR'S NOTE

Thanks for all the great reviews!

I've got more adventures for Tyson and JD. Stay tuned.

If you liked this book, let me know with a review on Amazon.

Hope you are well during this challenging time. Thanks for reading!

—*Tripp*

# TYSON WILD

Wild Ocean

Wild Justice

Wild Rivera

Wild Tide

Wild Rain

Wild Captive

Wild Killer

Wild Honor

Wild Gold

Wild Case

Wild Crown

Wild Break

Wild Fury

Wild Surge

Wild Impact

Wild L.A.

Wild High

Wild Abyss

Wild Life

Wild Spirit

# CONNECT WITH ME

I'm just a geek who loves to write. Follow me on Facebook.

www.trippellis.com

Made in the USA
Monee, IL
06 August 2021

75075691R00159